A split s[illegible]
through the night, [illegible]
flank. With a cry laced with shock and pain, he went down, unable to run any longer. His soft grey fur was already matted with blood, and panic overtook him as he wondered if he were going to die in his shifted state. He tried to crawl away but knew it was futile, as his keen ears could already hear the thundering footsteps approaching of the one who'd shot him. Soft whimpers escaped him, and he would have had tears in his eyes—if he'd been human.

Deep despair tugged at him, and he cursed himself for making it all the way to the wilds of Alaska only to be shot by an over-zealous gunman who was moving in on *his* wife. Rogan growled at the thought, baring his teeth at his own frustration.

His tail thumped on the ground as he tried yet again to pull himself further along, yet he had no luck. His leg was useless.

"Rogan." A familiar voice whispered to him from the foliage. *"Christ, Rogan, shift! SHIFT!"*

That was Wade's voice. What had he said to do—shit? Rogan's head was reeling, but he heard Wade's voice hiss at him once again.

"Shift, you bastard!"

Rogan understood that time.

Wondering to himself why he should ever again do anything Wade suggested, Rogan took his advice and slowly shifted his body from a wolf into a human. The pain in his leg was sheer agony, and he cried out when he tried to move.

Within seconds, the gunman was upon him; Rogan could hear the man's sharp intake of breath. Leaning his forehead on the cold snow, Rogan could do no more than surrender, hoping the man had more honor than to shoot him in the back.

"Jesus, Mister. You okay?"

"No, you idiot! I've been shot!"

Champagne Books Presents

B*E*A*S*T* Of Burden

By

Rebecca Goings

Champagne Books
www.champagnebooks.com

ISBN 978-1-897445-29-7
February 2007

Produced in Canada

Champagne Books
#35069-4604 37 ST SW
Calgary, AB T3E 7C7
Canada

Dedication

This book is dedicated to the best darn editor on the face of the planet: Joyce Scarbrough. Without your patience and guidance, I truly do not believe I would be the writer I am today. Much love and hugs!

One

Somewhere in the Alaskan Wilderness

A split second after the shotgun blast echoed through the night, hot fire sliced through Rogan Wolfe's left flank. Uttering a cry laced with shock and pain, he went down, unable to run any longer. His soft grey fur was already matted with blood, and panic overtook him as he wondered if he was going to die in his shifted state. He tried to crawl away but knew it was futile, as his keen ears could already hear the approaching footsteps of the one who'd shot him. Soft whimpers escaped him, and he would have had tears in his eyes—if he'd been human.

Deep despair tugged at him, and he cursed himself for making it all the way to the wilds of Alaska only to be shot by an over-zealous gunman who was moving in on *his* wife. Rogan growled at the thought, baring his teeth at his own frustration. His tail thumped on the ground as he tried yet again to pull himself further along, yet he had no luck. His leg was useless.

"Rogan." A familiar voice whispered to him from the foliage. *"Christ, Rogan, shift! SHIFT!"*

That was Wade's voice. What had he said to do—shit? Rogan's head was reeling, but he heard Wade's voice hiss at him once again.

"Shift, you crazy bastard!"

Rogan understood that time. Wondering to himself why he should ever again do anything Wade suggested, Rogan took his advice and slowly shifted his body from a wolf into a human. The pain in his leg was sheer agony, and he cried out when he tried to move.

Within seconds, the gunman was upon him; Rogan knew because he could hear the man's sharp intake of breath. Pressing his forehead into the cold snow, Rogan could do no more than surrender, hoping the man had more honor than to shoot him in the back.

"Jesus, mister. You okay?"

"No, you idiot!" Rogan's teeth were clenched as he said the words, trying to keep a civil tongue in his mouth. "I've been shot!"

"I'm sorry! I was shooting at a wolf and… I must have accidentally—"

Rogan heard a commotion in the bushes before he saw Wade running toward them. "Is everything all right? I heard gunfire!"

Shaking his head at his friend, Rogan sighed as he closed his eyes. Wade was almost as stupid as Justin had been. He should have stayed hidden! There was no reason for him to come running to Rogan's rescue.

"I… he's been shot!" The gunman sounded panicked. "Why the hell is he naked?"

"Don't worry about that now!" Wade exclaimed, shrugging out of his coat and tossing it to Rogan on the ground. "Help me get him to shelter. Looks like it might snow again."

The two men hefted Rogan between them once he had the coat firmly around his hips, making him grunt in pain.

"What are you doing?" Rogan demanded, resting his

flashing eyes on his old friend.

"We're helping you, sir," Wade said, glancing at the man holding the gun. "Just relax."

"Relax?" Rogan cried out when Wade's leg bumped his, making shards of pain shoot throughout the four corners of his body.

"I see lights up ahead!" Wade said, pointing to the house Rogan had been circling in his shifted state a few minutes earlier.

"That's my… girlfriend's house," the gunman said.

Rogan's head turned toward him. The man wore a heavy jacket and a furry hat, but all Rogan could concentrate on was his pulsing jugular. If he weren't in so much damned pain, he would have shifted to teach this man a lesson. Marlie wasn't *his* girlfriend—she belonged to Rogan! He growled low in his throat.

The man must have heard it, because as they limped toward the house, he glanced up only to shudder at the look in Rogan's eyes. "Don't you worry about a thing, mister," he said in a shaky voice. "We'll take care of you."

Rogan opened his mouth to say something, but he grunted when he felt a jab in his ribs. Whipping his head about, his gaze locked with Wade's, who adamantly shook his head a few times. Rogan narrowed his eyes and growled again, telling Wade without words that he wasn't too happy.

But within a few moments, nothing else mattered. There, on the porch step of the quaint house nestled amidst the snow and trees, stood Marlie Silver, the woman Rogan had been dreaming about for weeks at the B*E*A*S*T* compound. The woman he'd come all the way to Alaska to find.

His wife.

~ * ~

Marlie seethed when she finally caught sight of Kevin in the trees, but he wasn't alone. He and another man were flanking a third, helping him limp along to the house.

"Marlie, open the door!" Kevin called out, his warm breath puffing in the chilled air.

"What happened?" she asked, eyeing the man who was limping and wondering why he was wearing nothing but a jacket tied precariously around his waist.

"I shot him," Kevin replied. "I was aiming for that damned wolf but got this guy instead."

Marlie gasped as she flew to the door, opening it wide to allow the men to pass through. "I told you not to shoot it!"

Stumbling back into the warmth of the house, Marlie waited until all three men were through the door before she closed it behind them. That's when she noticed the blood.

"Kevin, he's bleeding everywhere!"

"I know, damn it!" Kevin yelled, glaring over his shoulder.

Marlie ran into the bathroom down the hall, rummaging underneath the sink for her first aid kit. Fortunately, it was chock full of gauze. Being a vet and living in the wilderness made her prepared for anything. More than once, she'd nursed wild animals back to health. Now her supplies were needed for a full-grown man. She just hoped she had enough.

Damn Kevin and his damned macho bullshit! So what if there was a wolf outside? They lived in Alaska, for Heaven's sake. Wolves and bears were a way of life. But the moment he'd seen the creature out the window, he'd grabbed her grandfather's old Winchester shotgun and ran down the porch steps before she could stop him.

Shaking her head, she knew now was not the time to berate him for wanting to play hero. A man was shot, and she had to worry about him for the moment. Dashing back into the living room, she could see they'd moved the injured man into her dining room, laying him down on her expensive dinner table. Marlie stopped in her tracks, trying desperately not to scream that the table was solid mahogany when she saw that the wounded man had bled all over it.

"Kevin," she began, but he held up his hand to stop her.

"I'll buy you a new one, woman! Just give me the damned gauze!"

Marlie stood there with her mouth wide open ready to blast him with her indignation, when suddenly the man on the table lifted his hand.

"Don't you talk to her that way," he said, his gritty voice tugging at her memory.

Had she heard it before? Who was this man?

The stranger who had helped Kevin and the injured man into the house licked his lips nervously and chuckled, as if trying to break the ice. Swallowing hard, Marlie made her way to the table where Kevin snatched the kit out of her hands, already trying to stem the man's bleeding with a dishrag.

The man on the table cried out, making Marlie jump. She *did* recognize his voice. But… it wasn't possible! Inching closer to the table, she gazed over the man's chest and into his face, gasping while her eyes filled with tears.

"Oh my God…"

She covered her mouth with her hand, rooted to the spot, unable to move. Her skin crawled and the room whirled about her head.

"Marlie, call 911!" Kevin commanded.

"No!" the other stranger shouted, glancing back and forth between Kevin and Marlie. "No, we cannot have the police out here."

"But he's been shot!" Kevin's voice echoed in Marlie's ears.

The stranger continued to argue with him. Talk of blood loss and lawsuits filled the air, but Marlie wasn't listening. Her entire world was focused on the man lying on her table who was staring back at her with such intensity it made her suck in her breath. She couldn't break his eye contact even if she'd wanted to.

Drawing a ragged breath, she uttered, "Dear God. *Matthew?*"

Two

Marlie ran to the kitchen sink, the contents of her stomach threatening to revisit her. It was Matthew, but that wasn't possible. How was he there? How was he *alive*?

"What's the matter with you?" she heard Kevin's voice yell from behind her.

Clutching the countertop, her knuckles went white and hot tears trailed down her face. She was afraid to turn around, afraid to face the man on her table. She had to be mistaken. There was *no way* that injured man could be Matthew! She'd buried her husband herself almost two years ago.

"Marlie," Kevin called out once more. "Call the damned paramedics!"

"No!"

That *was* Matthew's voice. She'd know it anywhere. The voice that had the power to turn her insides to mush; the voice that had whispered his love for her on many a starlit night. Marlie couldn't breathe.

"Are you insane, mister?" Kevin exclaimed. "You've been shot!"

"I'm aware of that!" His voice sent another tremor

through Marlie's body. "Don't worry about me. I'll manage."

Turning slowly, Marlie's breath came in short gasps as she continued to clutch the countertop behind her. The man on the table was now sitting up, resting his weight on his elbows as he gazed at her through what had to be a cloud of pain.

It *was* Matthew. Marlie would bet her life on it.

"Do you know this guy?" Kevin asked, looking back and forth between them.

"I… I don't know," she managed to say past the lump in her throat.

"But you called him Matthew."

Marlie could only nod while her heart raced. She knew she must be as white as a sheet, but as hard as she tried, she couldn't take her eyes off the man on the table.

"Then who is he?"

Turning his gaze to Kevin, the man said, "I'm her husband."

Silence descended on them as Kevin's eyes widened. "But her husband is dead."

"As you can clearly see, I am very much alive, and I would appreciate it if you'd stop jabbing my wounds!" Sitting up fully, he pushed Kevin's hands away from the dishrag, reaching for the gauze himself inside the first aid kit.

"What the hell?" Kevin demanded. "What's going on here, Marlie?"

"I don't know!" she exclaimed, turning her tearful eyes on him. "I don't know what the hell is going on. Matthew is dead!"

"Clearly I'm not," the man said, grunting when he shifted his weight on the table. "But your *boyfriend* here almost made it a reality."

"My what?" Marlie glared at Kevin. "My

boyfriend?"

Kevin chuckled nervously. "I can explain, Marlie."

"This man is *not* my boyfriend."

"Marlie—"

"We're just friends, Kevin. How could you say that you're my boyfriend?"

"Well, I… I—"

"Hey, I'm bleeding here! Little help?"

Marlie's anger compelled her to push away from the kitchen sink. Shoving Kevin out of the way, she grabbed the gauze herself.

"There's one way to find out if you really are Matthew," she said, giving the injured man a glare as well. "My husband had a scar on his inner thigh from climbing over a barbed wire fence when he was a teenager." Grabbing the jacket, she lifted it up only to jump back at the man's loud protest as he smacked it out of her hand.

"Now wait just a minute!" he said. "I may be your husband, but we've only just met!"

Marlie slapped his hands away in return. "Do you want me to call the cops?"

The man's dark eyes flashed gold momentarily, and a bolt of fear raced up Marlie's spine. He set his jaw and looked at the ceiling.

"Go for it, babe," he finally said. "I'm sure you've seen it all before."

Grinding her teeth, Marlie once again lifted the jacket and gasped. There on the inner flesh of his right thigh was the long white scar she knew so well. Images of herself licking that very scar came back to her in a rush. She'd kissed him there when they'd first made love, telling him that it didn't matter, that she'd found him sexy regardless of his scar.

Marlie glanced back at his face, unable to find words to speak. Her mouth was dry and more tears filled her eyes.

The man's face softened, and he almost reached out to touch her hair, but he dropped his hand before he did.

"It's me, Marlie," he said gently. "And we've got a *lot* to talk about."

~ * ~

Rogan watched as Marlie's eyes filled with tears. Her face was finally in front of him, the very face that had haunted his dreams for weeks. Yet, as hard as he tried, he couldn't remember anything about their lives together—falling in love with her, their courtship, their wedding. The only memory he had was of making love to her underneath the light of the moon. Even thinking about it made his body tighten with desire.

"Where have you been?" Marlie's stricken voice pierced his head, and guilt overcame him. All this time she'd been alone, thinking he was dead. How could he possibly know what kind of hell she'd endured? He could see some of her pain shining through her eyes.

"Wait, wait, wait." Kevin's voice broke through his thoughts. "You *faked* your death?"

"I didn't fake a damn thing," Rogan said with a growl, turning his gaze toward the irritating man. "I was *abducted*, and now I can't remember anything about the man I used to be. Nothing but *you,* Marlie." He looked back at her and she blushed.

"This is ridiculous," Kevin said. "Abducted? Then who the hell faked your death? Don't tell me you believe this garbage, Marlie!"

"Kevin, I think it's time for you to go," she said.

"No. I'm not leaving you here with these strange men. Not until we get to the bottom of this."

"There is no *we*," Marlie said, glaring at Kevin. "Regardless of what's going on, this man is Matthew Silver—my husband—and I want to have some time alone with him."

Kevin's face burned a bright red, but he didn't argue. Setting the shotgun by the door, he turned and said, "I'm going to be calling on you later this evening, and I'll come by tomorrow to check on you." Glancing at Rogan, he pointed his finger and said, "Don't even think about trying anything, mister. If you hurt her, you're gonna die. Again."

The door slammed behind him, rattling a few decorative plates hanging on the walls. Silence filled the room as Marlie glanced at Wade.

"And who are you?"

Clearing his throat, Wade held out his hand. "My name is Wade McAllister. I'm a friend of Rogan's. Of your husband's."

"Rogan?" Marlie looked confused.

"That's what they call me," Rogan said, trying to ignore his pounding headache. "Rogan Wolfe."

"They? Why would *they* call you by your middle name?"

"My middle name? You mean Rogan is my *real* name?"

Marlie nodded and sniffled. "You truly don't remember?"

Rogan shook his head. "I wish I did. All I can remember clearly is the past two years, and…"

"And what?" she asked when he paused.

"It's nothing."

"No, tell me." With her soft words, Marlie laid her hand on his. The contact of her skin sent a shiver throughout his body. The way she looked at him made him lower his eyes.

"I can remember… you… and me. Outside at night. Making love."

Marlie gasped and looked away.

"I'm sorry if I upset you."

"Upset me? Matthew, you just suddenly reappeared

in my life. Of course I'm more than a little upset! I don't know what to think—hell, what to *believe* anymore. I went to your funeral. I said goodbye to you! Yet here you are, clearly alive and well, and I had no goddamn idea!"

"You have every right to be angry, Marlie," he told her. "But don't be mad at me. *I* didn't leave you. Those bastards at B*E*A*S*T* took me from you. They did horrible things, even told you I was dead in order to keep me. But I escaped them, and I knew I had to find you, to tell you that I'm not truly dead. I had to let you know."

"What do you expect me to do? Fall into your arms?"

"No, but you have a right to know that you're still married."

Marlie swallowed hard. "You… you said someone named Beast abducted you?"

"Not someone, an agency. B*E*A*S*T* is an acronym; it stands for Bio-Engineering to Attain Shift Transformation."

"What does that mean?"

Wade decided to jump in at that moment. "Uh, I hate to bring you two back to the issue at hand, but Rogan still has a few shot pellets in his leg that we need to remove."

Marlie sighed as she rubbed her eyes. "I'm a vet; I only work on animals."

Rogan stared hard at her. "Marlie," he began, "if it will help you get this shot out of me, I'll shift for you, but you've got to promise me you won't freak out."

He could smell her sudden unease at his words. "What are you talking about?"

"You want to know what B*E*A*S*T* means? I'll do better than tell you. I'll *show* you."

Rogan slowly began to shift right on the dining room table until nothing was left of his human form. His golden eyes stared into Marlie's, hoping to God she'd understand

and not scream her head off. But once he was fully transformed into a wolf, Marlie squealed and jumped away from the table.

"Jesus, Mary, and Joseph!" she shouted.

Three

Marlie stumbled back into the living room, almost knocking over the lamp on the end table by the couch. Her mouth dropped open as more tears filled her eyes. Instead of Matthew lying on the table, a wounded wolf now regarded her with tame, golden eyes.

"What the hell is that?" she screamed, pointing her finger, unable to move. "Where's Matthew?"

Wade swallowed hard and took a step toward her. She moved away from him only to once again come up hard against the end table.

"He's right here," Wade said, running his fingers through his hair and glancing back at the wolf. "The B*E*A*S*T* agency stole all of us from our lives and brainwashed us. Nobody knows who we used to be in our lives before. The B*E*A*S*T* scientists mutated us. They played God with our genetic code and made us what we are. We're shifters. We can become certain animals. Rogan… I mean *Matthew,* is a timber wolf."

Marlie's eyes widened as her heart threatened to beat right out of her chest. "*You* can do this too?" she asked in a small voice, suddenly glancing around for the shotgun Kevin had propped against the wall near the door.

"Yes, I can," Wade said, holding up his hands. "But we won't hurt you. Besides, I'm not a wolf. I'm a cougar."

"Is that supposed to make me feel better?" she shrieked, clutching the sides of her head as if to hold herself together.

"Look, Marlie," Wade said, "I can smell your fear, and I want you to know you have nothing to be afraid of. We won't hurt you. Rogan had fleeting memories of a woman, and when we looked up his classified file on the B*E*A*S*T* computers, we found out about you. He wanted to come and find you. What this agency has done to *all* of us is unforgivable."

Marlie couldn't stop the tears from falling. "Dear God," she whispered, crumpling to the floor. "They took Matthew from me and made him a monster?"

Wade nodded, kneeling next to her. "They made all of us monsters. Made us endure gruesome torture and stole whatever memories we had. But some of us could remember flashes—bits and pieces of who we used to be. Some of us have escaped. Rogan and I included."

Marlie took a deep breath and closed her eyes, then she took another deep breath and tried her hardest to calm herself down.

"We need to get him to a… a doctor. He's injured," she said once she opened her eyes again.

"*You're* a doctor."

"I'm a *vet.*"

"Right now, *he's* a wolf. Marlie, please. I know you don't know me, but you do know him. We cannot afford to have the authorities here. We've escaped from the B*E*A*S*T* compound, but they're still looking for us. We can't risk bringing attention to ourselves. B*E*A*S*T* is bigger than anyone first expected. They're sure to have their hand in every pie. If we call the police, they'll know and be here within the hour to 'clean everything up'."

"What does that mean?" Marlie shuddered by the look in Wade's eyes.

"They'd kill us all."

Marlie gasped as her stomach lurched inside of her.

"Rogan and I are pretty high up on B*E*A*S*T*'s most-wanted list," Wade went on. "Before we escaped, we freed all the other shifters. They're going to be searching for us with a fine-tooth comb. Please, Marlie, if you can do something for Rogan…" Wade let the sentence hang.

After a few moments of silence, Marlie looked out the window and gasped. "The wolf outside, the one Kevin saw. That was… *Matthew*?"

Wade hung his head. "Yes. I… *may* have suggested to him to go up to the house and see what you were up to. Rogan wanted to know if you were remarried or if you'd moved on. He didn't want to interfere with your life if you'd found someone new. So instead of slinking around your house in human form, he thought it would be better to appear as a wolf, so you wouldn't freak out."

"Well, I'm freaking out right now!"

A yip came from the table, and Marlie looked over Wade's shoulder to see the wolf staring right at her. He yipped one more time and wagged his tail. She shivered. Was it true what Wade said? Was her husband truly a shifter? How was it even possible? And who had she *really* buried two years ago?

She didn't think long on it. Her stomach roiled once more, and she knew any further thought about the man in Matthew's grave would make her retch right there and then. She'd been told Matthew had died in a terrible car accident. The car had caught on fire, and they'd had to identify his body through his dental records. Another shiver raced down her spine. Obviously, that had been a lie.

"I… I don't have anything to sedate him with."

"That's all right," Wade said. "I'll hold him down."

The wolf growled at him and bared its teeth.

"He can understand you?" she asked in awe.

"Yes, we can understand language in our shifted state. We can also think as humans. But our DNA says we're one hundred percent the creature we've become—a 'perk' B*E*A*S*T* wove into their shifters."

"Why would they make such creatures?" Marlie asked, moving closer to the table. With a shaking hand, she reached out and touched the wolf's tail.

"It's probably better if you don't ask that question," Wade said.

Marlie shuddered. "You're right. I don't want to know." Clearing her throat, she grabbed the first aid kit. Fortunately, there was a scalpel, needle-nose tweezers and a needle and thread. "I'll try to be as gentle as I can," she whispered to the wolf, stroking its coat. "I don't have all the tools I usually use for this kind of thing."

The wolf whined and laid down its head. Good to his word, Wade stretched out his body over the wolf's.

"Don't worry, old buddy," he said. "I'm sure Marlie knows what she's doing."

The wolf growled but didn't move. With a shaking hand, Marlie operated, pulling out five shot pellets from its flank. More than once, the animal jumped and howled.

"I'm so sorry, Matthew," she said through gritted teeth. "Usually when I do this, my patient is knocked out."

It took longer than she anticipated due to his thrashing, but once she'd finished, she tossed the shot pellets into the trash. "He'll have to… um, shift in order for me to stitch him up."

The wolf began to change shape, once again morphing its body into that of her husband. Watching him transform raised the hair on the back of her neck. His soft grey fur disappeared, replaced by smooth skin. His legs grew longer and thicker, as did his arms, and his snout shrank into a human nose and mouth.

"Sweet Jesus," he said, still growling. "That hurt like a son of a bitch!"

Opening her fridge, Marlie pulled out a few ice cube trays. "We'll numb your skin before I suture you. That should help with some of the pain."

"Got any whiskey?"

"No."

"Tequila?"

"No."

"Vodka?"

"I'm not a big drinker, you know that!"

"Actually, I don't," he said.

Marlie lowered her gaze and felt her heart lurch inside of her. He was right; he didn't remember. The man she had once adored more than life itself didn't know a damn thing about her. With a forlorn sigh, Marlie opened her cabinet.

"I... I like Midori Sours. I'm afraid Midori is all I have."

"I'll take it." Rogan reached out his hand, his fingers beckoning her.

Biting her lip, Marlie crossed the kitchen and handed it to him, watching as he opened the bottle and downed the contents. He cried out once the ice touched his skin, but she didn't let up.

"Do you want this to hurt more?"

"Hell no!"

"Then quit your bitching!"

Rogan was silent for a moment before he raised his eyebrows and chuckled, glancing at his friend. "I knew I would have married a firecracker."

Wade hid his smile behind his hand while he helped Marlie with the ice. She blushed hotly, refusing to meet her husband's piercing gaze.

Four

Snow began to fall in the darkness beyond the window. Marlie had started a fire in the massive stone fireplace that took up almost one entire wall of the living room. Soon, the fire warmed the house. Now she stood gazing out the window, watching the snowflakes and feeling a cold numbness inside her heart.

She'd purchased this very house with Matthew four years ago, their wedding present to each other. She could even remember how giddy he'd been as he'd spun her in his arms once escrow had closed. Their very first night in the house, they'd built a roaring fire—not unlike the one she'd just lit—and they'd made love long into the night. Marlie could already feel more tears behind her eyes.

After Matthew's impromptu surgery on her dining room table, he'd asked her if she had any clothing for him to wear. Fortunately for him, she did. She hadn't been able to bear throwing away her husband's old things, so instead of giving them away to Goodwill, she'd tucked them into the closet of the guest room. Her family and friends had no idea, and they'd be shocked to learn she sometimes wandered in there late at night to smell his old shirts, even though his scent had long since vanished.

Marlie had loved her husband dearly. He was the love of her life. Hearing of his death had almost destroyed her. She'd sequestered herself in their house during the following months and only emerged to attend his funeral and go to work. She'd also visited his grave on many occasions. Marlie had even once considered selling the house, but she'd decided it was better to live with the old memories rather than pretend they had never happened.

Matthew's loud yelp from the couch cut into her pensive thoughts. She turned from the sill only to see Wade trying to dress him in his old clothes.

"I think it's best if he doesn't wear the jeans," she said, smiling when both men scowled at her. "You don't want to aggravate the wounds any more than you have to."

Matthew pushed Wade away and buttoned the shirt himself, looking quite handsome in the blue plaid. That had been Marlie's favorite shirt of his so long ago, and seeing him in it now took her breath away. Black boxers completed his ensemble.

He glanced up at her from where he sat, and her heart slammed to life. Matthew was alive! She could hardly believe it. But he didn't remember her. How cruel for the fates to decide to return the man of her dreams, only to have his memories vanish like the withering grass.

"Your hair is longer," she said, just to have something to say.

"Is it?" Matthew lifted his hand to his head.

"Yeah."

Wade plopped down onto the recliner next to the fire and stretched out. "Got any pictures?"

"I do." She had boxes of pictures of him. But she'd be damned if she would tell him she went through them once a week.

"Show me."

The phone rang as Marlie started to leave, and she squealed and jumped at the same time.

"Don't answer it!" Wade called out.

Looking at her caller ID, Marlie groaned. "It's Kevin. If I don't pick up, he'll come back out here."

"Answer it," Rogan said.

Grabbing the receiver, she pressed the talk button. "Hello?"

"Are you all right?"

"I'm fine, Kevin."

"I'm worried about you with those strange men. Are you sure you don't want me there?"

"I'm sure. They're good men. They haven't hurt me at all. In fact, I just pulled the shot pellets out of Matthew."

"I don't like this one bit. It's too weird that your dead husband just suddenly pops up out of nowhere."

Marlie sighed and bit her lip. "I know, but I have to get to the bottom of this."

"I'm still coming over in the morning, Marlie. Expect me around nine."

"All right," she conceded, knowing he'd only race back over tonight if she argued.

"If you need anything—anything at all—call me. Doesn't matter what time it is."

"All right!" she said with another sigh. "Look, Kevin. I'm going to let you go. Have a good night." Without waiting to hear him say goodbye, she hung up the phone.

"Are these *his* clothes?" Matthew's voice was low, but she could hear the contempt from where she stood.

Whirling around to face him, she shook her head. "No," she said.

"Then who do they belong to?"

Marlie swallowed hard as she wrung her hands in front of her. "You." He looked shocked, so she pressed on. "I never threw anything away after you died. I kept it all. My friends and family tried to get me to date again, which is why Kevin's hanging around. I went on a blind date with him three months ago—one of my co-workers set it up. We never hit it off romantically, but he likes to check up on me once in awhile. Says a woman shouldn't be all by herself in the wilds of Alaska, seeing as how this house is on a dirt road so far off the beaten path. I know he wants more, but…" She shrugged. "I'm just not ready."

Rogan stared at her for a few silent moments, making her shift her weight from foot to foot.

"I'm sorry I'm rambling," she said. "Let me go get those pictures."

With that, Marlie scurried out of the room, relieved to get away from her husband's intense eyes.

~ * ~

"She's still in love with you." Wade whispered his words with a half grin on his face. His arms were folded behind his head as he lifted a leg over the arm of the easy chair.

Rogan sighed, staring down the hallway where she'd disappeared. He could smell her scent: it was one of uncertainty, but it was also laced with desire. She'd been shocked to see him dressed in this shirt, and his body had tightened at the look in her eyes.

Marlie was a beautiful woman with her shoulder-length chocolate brown hair. Her dark eyes were almost the same color brown—deep pools that made him wonder how often he'd lost himself gazing into them. Her smile was soft and lit up her face. He wanted to see that smile more often.

Rogan couldn't even imagine what kind of shock this must be for her, learning that he was alive, that his death had been faked. Not only had B*E*A*S*T* stolen the last two years of *his* life, they'd stolen *hers* as well. His anger burned hot inside him at the thought. How dare those bastards do that to this stunning woman!

"It's been two years, Wade."

"Doesn't matter," Wade said as he closed his eyes. "She's got it bad. She's still got your clothes if that gives you a clue. And you might not have seen it, but the way she looks at you… I'd lay money down that she's still in love with you. Not to mention her scent—"

"Talk about her scent again, and I'll rip out your throat, Cougar."

Wade chuckled but didn't open his eyes. "It seems as if the attraction is a two-way street."

"Of course I'm attracted to her," Rogan said, exasperated. "She's the one thing I can remember from my life before. But I'm not going to go jumping into anything foolish, even if the woman is my wife."

"Why the hell not?" Wade asked, finally cracking open his eyes. "You've got a license; she's *yours*."

"The man she fell in love with is *dead*." Rogan grunted while trying to get comfortable.

"But *you* aren't. You have a second chance here, buddy. Don't let it slip through your fingers."

Marlie emerged from one of the bedrooms down the hall with a large photo album. Laying it on the coffee table, she said, "Here you go."

Rogan glanced up at her and smelled her unease. Patting the cushion next to him, he said, "Sit here and show me. I want to hear whatever stories you have to tell."

Marlie licked her lips but sat diligently, her back as stiff as a board.

"I won't bite," he said, teasing her.

"I… I know," she whispered as she grabbed the book. "But I'm just… overwhelmed right now."

With a nod, Rogan sat back against the cushions and watched as she opened the cover of the album.

"This is our wedding album," she said. "We were married four years ago in April."

On the first page was a picture of her, so very beautiful in a white, flowing gown. She was standing in many different poses, smiling at the photographer through a soft camera filter. She looked so happy; almost radiant.

"Wow," Rogan said, honestly taken aback by how beautiful she was. Her hair was swept off her neck into a cascading array of ringlets while all sorts of small flowers were woven into it. Her bouquet was made of deep red roses with white roses as accents, and her train trailed out behind her majestically.

"You're gorgeous," he whispered as he caressed one of the photos. "And so happy."

"I was about to marry the man of my dreams," she said, then looked as if she regretted it. Her cheeks flamed red as she turned the page. "Here you are."

Shock flooded through him. It was him only younger—in a military dress uniform.

"You were in the Marines." Marlie's soft voice made the hair on his arms stand on end.

"I know."

She gave him a look, probably wondering how he knew that.

"I found out when I looked at my file on the B*E*A*S*T* computers."

With a nod, Marlie stroked the photo, and his heart slammed to life inside of him. She still cared, after all this time.

"You were a captain, and so very proud to be serving your country."

"I look pretty happy too."

"You were. Told one and all that you couldn't wait to marry me. I'd said yes and you weren't about to let me get away."

Rogan glanced up at Wade, who cocked his eyebrow. Giving him a sour look, Rogan glanced back down at the pictures. As the pages turned, Rogan's heart fell. He couldn't remember any of this. It was his wedding day! One of the most important days of his life, and his memories were gone.

As Marlie turned to the last page, there were a few candid shots of them together—one cheek to cheek and another of them kissing. Marlie's fingers were anchored in his hair, and he held her close to him. He stared at the photo for a few silent moments.

"I wish I could remember this," he whispered, touching the picture right where their lips met. He turned his gaze to Marlie, and she visibly shuddered.

"I do," she said. "You made my heart sing."

"I'm so sorry, Marlie. For everything. I'm sorry it worked out this way between us."

Her eyes shone with unshed tears. "I am too." She grabbed something that was on a chain underneath her shirt.

"What's that?" he asked.

Marlie looked as if she were reluctant to show him. But after a moment of silence, she pulled it out. "My wedding ring."

The diamonds sparkled in the firelight as she held it up.

"You never took it off?"

Marlie sniffled. "It took me a year to take it off my finger. Looks like it's taken me another year to take it off of my neck."

She looked at him once more, and all he wanted to do was lean over and kiss her despite the pain in his leg. She'd endured so much, and it was obvious that she still loved him. Deeply.

"If I could take it all back, I would," he said.

One silent tear fell from her eyes and slid down her cheek.

"You came back to me," she whispered. "But you

don't remember me. Things will never be the same between us, Matthew. You may still be alive, but the man I loved died two years ago."

When she stood from the couch and retreated into the bedroom, Rogan suddenly felt empty and cold. Damn, this wasn't going to be easy.

Five

It was late. The antique clock on Marlie's mantel ticked incessantly. Rogan couldn't go to sleep no matter how hard he tried. They'd eaten earlier when Marlie had suggested she make some sandwiches for everyone. The food had been eaten in near silence. If it hadn't been for Wade and his big mouth, Rogan and Marlie would have had nothing to talk about.

Wade had told her all about their escape from the B*E*A*S*T* compound and their friend Noah, who could shift into a white tiger. But the memories of those days came back to haunt Rogan. He had been the one to free the shifters from their cells, and they had ruthlessly killed the guards he'd chained to the fence. He hadn't even been thinking about what the fate of the guards might be when he'd cuffed them to the chain link fence in order to keep them out of his way, but the memories of their screams ripped through his head. Rogan shuddered. No man deserved to die like that—a meal for hungry, vengeful shifters.

Tossing and turning on the couch did nothing to ease the ache in his leg, and he rubbed the bandages. B*E*A*S*T* had made sure all of their experiments were fast healers. He knew he didn't have to live with the pain for too much longer. But right now, his leg was on fire.

Rogan had seen Marlie get him some Tylenol earlier from her kitchen cabinet, so he stood precariously and hobbled into the kitchen to get himself some more. Just as he popped a few into his mouth and took a long drag from the glass of water he'd poured, he could hear the muffled sounds of sobbing.

It was Marlie.

Wade had retired down the hall, saying he was content to sleep in the guest room. Rogan had opted to sleep on the couch, not wanting to move more than necessary. But now that his keen ears could hear Marlie's crying, he couldn't find it within himself to merely lie back down and ignore it.

After stumbling down the hallway, he stopped at her door and could hear every one of her cries. She was trying not to be too loud, he could tell. She was probably using her pillow to muffle the sounds. But the muted scent of her pain wafted through the door, and it pierced his heart. No matter what he'd been through, he was still her husband, and that truth was what prompted him to knock on her door. He should be the one to comfort her. He longed to make her smile.

Once he'd knocked, her crying stopped, and he could hear hurried footsteps.

"Go away." Marlie's voice was soft but harsh, nonetheless.

"Marlie, we need to talk," he said gently.

"Matthew, please…"

"Open the door." Rogan laid his head on the cool wood. "You're the only thing I can remember. Don't shut me out. I… need you."

"I can't let you in," she said, her voice and scent close. She must be just on the other side of the door herself.

"If I do, then… then…"

Rogan made the decision for her when he opened the door and hobbled into the room. Marlie stared at him in shock, giving him the second he needed to close the door behind him.

"What are you doing?" she gasped, backing away. She looked stunning in her long nightshirt that hung to the middle of her thighs. On the front was a picture of a kitten that said *Cats Rule*. He had to smile at that.

"We need to talk," he said again, leaning back against the door.

"You shouldn't be in here!"

"Wasn't this *our* room?" he asked, glancing around at the king-sized bed and huge closet doors. Another door led into a room on the far wall; he assumed that must be the master bath.

"Yes, but—"

He held up his hand. "Look, I know things have changed between us. But I just need to know if I can remember anything more. And I need your help to do that."

With a sigh, Marlie sat on the edge of her bed and crossed her arms. "You always were one of the most stubborn men I ever met."

He grinned, moving forward to sit next to her. He stretched out his injured leg in front of him and grunted.

"You shouldn't be walking on that," she said in a softer tone, concern in her eyes.

"I'll be all right," he said, glancing at her. "I'm a fast healer. We… we all are."

Marlie swallowed hard.

Rogan took a deep breath. "I have one memory before B*E*A*S*T* abducted me. I've already told you what it is."

Even in the dark, Rogan could tell he'd made her blush.

"Can you help me remember when that… happened?"

Marlie's voice wavered. "Um, it was probably on our honeymoon."

"Yeah?"

She nodded, her scent filled with sadness but also yearning. She still wanted him. He was sure of it.

"We went to Fiji and rented a private beach house. The first night we got there, we strolled along the beach and laid out our towels." As she was talking, her eyes had a faraway look in them. "The moon was out that night and with so many stars, it was like a diamond blanket in the sky. One thing led to another and…" Marlie shrugged and let the sentence hang. She quickly wiped away a few fresh tears.

"I vaguely remember that," Rogan said to fill the silence. "I remember you, the sky, and how…"

"How what?" she asked when he didn't finish.

Lifting his gaze back to hers, he said, "I remember how you tasted."

Judging by her reaction, she hadn't expected those to be his words. With a gasp, she stood and tried to walk away, but he grabbed her wrist before she could. The heat of her soft skin made his heart pound in his chest. As he pulled her closer, her bare legs rubbed against his, and he groaned at the contact.

"Matthew—"

"Call me Rogan," he said. "I don't remember Matthew. I don't remember anything… except you. Except that night."

She shuddered.

"Marlie," he whispered. "May I kiss you?"

Her eyes were wide as she stared at him.

"I need to remember more," he continued. "I need to know if what I *do* remember is real. Please."

Pulling her even closer, he circled his arms around

her waist.

"Please?" he asked again.

Marlie closed her eyes and sucked in her breath.

~ * ~

She must be mad. That's the only explanation that made sense. Here she was, back in her husband's arms where she'd dreamt of being on so many countless nights. She was shaking, her body trembling with desire. He wanted to kiss her, and God help her, she wanted to let him. But he was a freak now, a man able to shift into a wolf at will. Marlie felt as if she were inside some bizarre dream.

But, as his arms tightened around her, she licked her lips and raised her hands. Without thinking about what she was doing, she stroked his cheeks.

"God, I've missed you so much, Matthew," she whispered to him.

"Rogan," he corrected, pulling her down until she was sitting in his lap.

"Rogan," she said, running her fingers through his hair. He growled low in his throat. "We shouldn't do this."

"Why not?"

"We can't just pick up where we left off."

"No, we can't," he agreed, running his large hands up her thighs to help her straddle him. She gasped at the warmth of his palms, which shot sparks of electricity throughout her body.

"But we can start fresh," he said.

"You don't remember me," she whispered, bringing her eyes back to his. She caressed his cheek and tried desperately to keep her tears at bay. She'd cried so much in the past few hours that she felt drained.

"Yes I do," he countered, lifting his own hands up her sides to her shoulders. Once his hands found her neck, he pulled her closer until their faces were no more than a breath apart. "I want to remember more."

Marlie hovered just above his lips, not exactly sure what to do next. If she kissed him, she wasn't sure she'd be able to stop herself. She'd been too long without him. Already she could feel the bold arousal in his boxers pressing against her panties.

"Kiss me," he whispered, his words sounding almost like a prayer.

His hands found their way down her body to rest on her backside, pressing her against him sensually. The look in his eyes was too much. She had never been able to resist him, and now was no exception. She closed the gap between them and pressed her lips to his.

Instantly, he held her head to him, as if to keep her from pulling away. Marlie had meant to make their kiss a chaste one, but Rogan wouldn't have it. Once their lips touched, he leaned back on the bed, bringing her with him. She mewled in shock but only for a moment. Lying on top of him brought the bulge in his boxers closer to her center, rubbing against her deliciously. She couldn't help but rock back and forth, reveling in the feeling of him against her once again.

Like the aggressive man he always had been, his tongue forced her mouth open, sliding into her mouth and capturing her own. Marlie's nipples ached as she slowly rocked against him, feeling the fires of her desire grow hotter and more intense with every passing moment. She'd missed him too damn much to pull away. He tasted so good that she didn't ever want to let him go for fear of losing him again.

With a groan, Rogan released her mouth only to whisper roughly, "I remember, Marlie. God, I remember your taste!" He didn't give her a chance to answer before he was kissing her again, thrusting his hips up to meet her.

Marlie cried out when he suddenly rolled her over onto her back. He didn't miss a beat before covering her body with his. Nudging her knees apart, he settled between them as he nipped and sucked on her neck.

"Matthew… Rogan," she panted. "We can't. We can't…"

Instead of waiting for what she might say, he silenced her with his lips. She whimpered into his mouth but let him discover her body all over again. In the back of her mind, she knew it was madness. Jumping back into a sexual relationship too fast could doom their fragile bond—assuming they still had one.

But, dear God, she couldn't stop herself.

Before she knew it, she'd unbuttoned his shirt and was stroking his chest, making him surge against her even harder than before.

"I need you," he whispered in her ear. "Marlie, I need to remember you."

"We shouldn't do this," she managed to say, her hands contradicting her words as she brought his nipples to fine points.

"Do you want me to stop?"

His tongue flicked her earlobe as his teeth teased it as well, making her ache intensify. Marlie bit her own lips to keep herself from crying *no*. His dark eyes perused her face as he leaned his forehead against hers.

"I'll stop if you ask me to," he said.

He was pleading with her to let him continue; she could see it as plain as day. Her resolve was crumbling.

"I don't want to ruin anything by getting too close too soon."

Rogan shut his eyes tightly and sighed, his body trembling above her. "You're right. Damn it."

Rolling off her, he panted hard and glared at the ceiling. Marlie immediately felt empty without him in her arms. She seriously considered asking him to continue what he'd started. It was obvious he was trying hard to control his raging libido. Snuggling next to him, she laid her head on his shoulder.

"Rogan?"

"Yeah?" he said with a sigh, bringing his arm around her shoulders.

"Will you… Oh, never mind."

"What? Tell me."

Curling her arm around his neck, she whispered, "Will you stay with me? I've been so cold since… since…" Once again, tears burned her eyes. She almost rolled away from him, but his arm held her fast.

"I'll stay," he answered gently, pulling back the covers. She helped him swing his legs under them.

"It's so good to hold you again," she murmured, yawning.

Rogan didn't answer. He merely stroked her hair. Marlie had no idea if he remembered doing that so long ago on the nights they'd spent in each other's arms. But it was so good to feel it again that she snuggled close to him, content to be surrounded by his strength.

Within moments, she was sound asleep.

Five

Rogan jerked awake and glanced around the room, disoriented. Sunlight poured through the blue curtains on the window near the headboard, and the sweet scent of Marlie surrounded him, but she wasn't in the bed. He could hear the sound of the shower in the master bathroom.

Damn it, he was going to drive himself insane. Thoughts of what she must look like naked ripped through his head like a freight train. Instantly his body tightened, and he had to grab hold of the comforter to keep himself from flying off the bed.

Last night had been the best night's sleep he'd gotten in a long time. He'd been so warm and comfortable, holding Marlie in his arms; he'd slept like a rock. Now, however, he lamented the fact that his body was now as hard as a rock.

"Shit," he whispered to himself, swinging his legs over the edge of the bed. Rubbing his eyes, he merely sat there, wondering what the hell to do. The clock on the side table read 8:45 a.m. Good ol' what's-his-name was going to make an appearance in fifteen minutes. Rogan growled at the thought. Marlie had mentioned that her friend Kevin wanted to take their relationship to the next level. Even though Rogan had only been reunited with his wife for barely a day, he felt his protective instincts kick in.

Marlie was *his* mate—end of story, damn it.

Dear God, is she humming in there?

He swallowed hard, trying not to think about her soapy skin, but it was nearly impossible. He knew he'd probably seen her naked many times during his life before, but no matter how hard he tried, he couldn't conjure the image in his memory, and his curiosity got the better of him.

Standing from the bed, he limped over to the closed bathroom door and opened it. A wall of steam hit him in the face. Lucky for Rogan, the door didn't squeal on its hinges. The shower was a stall with an opaque glass door, so he could see the vague outline of Marlie's body through it. Growling at himself in the fogged up mirror, he made a split decision.

"I'm gonna regret this," he said under his breath.

He stepped out of his boxers and let his shirt fall to the floor. Bending over, he also unwrapped the bandages on his injured leg and threw them into the trash can. Already his wounds felt better. They were still an angry red underneath Marlie's stitches, but he was able to put more weight on his leg than the night before. It had been awhile since he'd showered, and he couldn't think of a better way to get clean than to share the shower with his extremely beautiful wife.

The moment he opened the stall door, Marlie squealed and turned around in fright, her body wet from head to toe. Her long dark hair clung to her back, and the water splashed over her skin in rivulets. Marlie's breasts were just the right size for his hands—if she'd let him touch her—and the patch of hair between her legs was neatly trimmed. She didn't even bother to cover herself, she merely chewed the inside of her lip.

Rogan had meant to step into the shower with her,

but now that he'd gotten an eyeful of her exquisite body, all he could do was stand there and stare. Marlie looked at his face as if she were too afraid to glance down at his own nakedness.

After a few moments of shocked silence, she said harshly, "What do you think you're doing?"

"I'm gonna join you, sweetheart," he said, finally finding his voice as he stepped into the stall.

Marlie swallowed hard. "This… this isn't a good idea."

"Oh?" he countered, raising a brow at her. "What better way for me to remember you than to touch every inch of you?"

She closed her eyes. "Dear Lord, Matt—I mean, Rogan. You're a stubborn man."

He had to grin at her. "Damn right, honey. Are you complaining?"

Marlie shook her head and finally looked down at him. She gasped at the proof of his desire. He grew harder just having her stare at him. With a groan, he pushed her against the tiles of the shower.

"Can I touch you?" he asked.

Rogan knew he was being bold by joining her in the shower, but he didn't want her to think she didn't have a choice. He wanted her to accept him back into her life, but he also wanted her to choose him for herself.

"Can I taste you?" He didn't even recognize his own husky voice. Her hands rested on his biceps as he leaned over her, the warm shower spray slicking his skin.

"Rogan—"

He placed a finger over her lips. "Yes or no," he said, giving her a look he hoped she could read. He was forcing the issue, but damn it, he had to remember her. He had to grab hold of the life he'd once had. And, looking down at her creamy skin once more, he had to put his mouth on her.

Marlie bit her lip but didn't break his eye contact. Her breathing was rapid, and he could smell her desire through the scent of her flowery soap. She ran her hands up his arms to his shoulders. Rogan thought he was going to burst if she didn't answer him soon.

"Yes," she finally whispered.

Without another word, his mouth was on hers, tasting hungrily. He could feel her fingers threading through his hair, and it enflamed him. Pressing closer, he made sure she could feel every hard inch of him. Damn, he'd never wanted anything more in his life than to be inside of her at that moment. Her breasts were crushed on his chest, and he couldn't help but moan at the contact.

Reaching between them, he grabbed hold of each of them, rubbing her nipples to fine points against his palms. Marlie gasped in his mouth but didn't let go of him. He felt a surge of satisfaction pulse through him at his victory.

"We can't do this standing up," she panted when his mouth left hers to trail down her neck. "Your leg…" She let the sentence hang, and he knew she was right, despite the fact that he felt a little better.

"Turn off the shower," he commanded softly, stepping away from her just enough for her to turn off the faucet. Opening the stall door behind him, he stepped out and pulled her with him. He kicked the glass door shut and pulled her down to the bathroom floor.

"Right here?" she asked as he lowered his body onto hers.

"The bed's too damn far away," he said, immediately attaching his mouth to her nipple. Marlie cried out and arched into him, holding his head down. Rolling it in his mouth, he growled with pleasure at her gasps, rasping her nipple against his tongue until he brought it to a peak. He used his teeth to tease her, tugging ever-so-gently before sucking it deeply into his mouth.

His hand wandered down her belly until it rested in the wetness he sought. Giving her other breast the same treatment with his mouth, his fingers began to circle the tender flesh between her legs. Within mere moments, Marlie cried out, pressing against him again and again.

"Ro-gan!" she exclaimed, shuddering at the same time.

"Already, sweetheart?" he asked with a cocky grin, pleased he'd brought her to her pleasure so quickly.

She didn't allow him to gloat for very long. Grabbing his hair, she pulled him back painfully to her mouth.

"Make love to me," she whispered against his lips.

"What about—"

"I don't care!" she said. "It's been too long. I don't want to think about it."

Pulling back as far as she would let him, he stared into her amazing brown eyes.

"Marlie, I'm not the same man you married. Are you sure you want—"

At that moment, Wade banged on the bedroom door. "Rogan! Jesus, Rogan, are you in there?"

With a growl, Rogan laid his forehead on Marlie's shoulder. His body was trembling as he teetered on the edge of deciding whether or not to plunge deeply into his wife's willing body.

"What is it!" he yelled.

"I heard a man's scream outside! It sounded as if… he was yelling for help."

Raising himself up onto his elbows, Rogan glanced at Marlie underneath him. "Oh my God."

"What?" Marlie caressed his face with concern.

"Your friend Kevin. He should have been here by now." He stood and helped her up. After grabbing his shirt and boxers, he opened the bathroom door but stopped long enough to give Marlie a rough kiss. "I'm taking a rain check on your request, sweetheart."

Marlie licked her lips. "Do you think something happened to Kevin?"

"I have no idea. But if Wade heard a scream outside, we've got to go investigate. The B*E*A*S*T* agency doesn't play games. Promise me you'll stay in this house."

Marlie nodded.

"Promise me," he repeated, grabbing hold of her chin.

"I promise. I'll stay put until you get back."

Rogan nodded, throwing on his clothing as he walked to the bedroom door.

"Rogan," she called out, making him turn around to face her once again.

His manhood pressed against his boxers at the sight of her. Damn, she was beautiful in all her glory.

"What?"

"Take my grandfather's shotgun with you. There are some shells in the kitchen drawer by the fridge."

Rogan nodded with a half-grin and walked out of the room.

Six

His belly was full. It had been a long time since he'd had a warm meal. His victim's screams had been music to his ears. Sean Ross grinned through the blood on his face as he glanced at the remains of the man who'd been driving up the dirt road to Marlie's house. Once he'd seen the truck coming his way, Sean hadn't been able to resist the gnawing hunger in his gut any longer.

He'd quickly undressed and shifted, smiling to himself that B*E*A*S*T* had engineered him to become a Kodiak grizzly, one of the most powerful creatures on the face of the Earth. With hunger on his mind, he'd stepped out in front of the beat-up Ford truck and stood on his hind legs, his fierce growl echoing through the woods.

Just as Sean knew he would, the terrified man in the truck had slammed on the brakes, the rear of the vehicle fishtailing. There was no way the man could make a fast getaway on the fresh powder of last night's snowfall. Once the truck had come to a complete stop, Sean bounded to the driver's side door, shifting just enough to rip the door off its hinges before returning to his grizzly state and dragging the man out of the truck's cabin.

The man never had a chance.

He'd screamed for his life and Sean had let him, knowing damn well that Rogan and Wade would be able to hear it in the house not too far away. Sean had ripped away the man's shirt and sank his teeth into his belly, rejoicing at the texture of the flesh in his mouth.

The man's screams had filled his ears while Sean ate him alive. The warmth of his blood had filled his mouth and slithered down his throat, and he hadn't been able to help but groan with pleasure. After a few moments, Sean had decided he'd had enough. He'd grabbed the man's throat in his mighty jaws and heard his neck break with a sickening snap.

Once his belly was full, Sean lumbered into the trees near where he'd tossed his clothing. He shifted and donned them again, wiping his bloody mouth and hands on the fabric. He had a plan, and it involved torturing Rogan in mind and body before finally killing him as Covington had ordered. And Sean was going to start with Rogan's pretty wife.

Grinning to himself, he slinked through the trees, thankful that Marlie's house was upwind from the man he'd just killed. His *friends* wouldn't be able to locate him by his smell until it was too late. From the cover of the woods, he watched as Rogan and Wade ran out of the house alone, probably to investigate the scream they'd just heard moments before. Sean had to chuckle at the shotgun Rogan gripped in his hand.

Marlie must still inside. Perfect.

~ * ~

Marlie's body trembled, but she didn't know if it was due to fear or desire. She'd quickly gotten dressed in a black sweater and blue jeans, still reeling from the orgasm that had rocked her not more than a few minutes before. She stopped a moment when she glanced into her jewelry box, but she grabbed the chain that held her wedding ring. As she clasped the necklace around her neck, she dropped it inside her sweater to rest against her skin. Her husband had come back to her—the least she could do was continue to wear the ring he'd given her so long ago.

Seeing Rogan open the shower door had startled her, but, in a way, she'd been relieved to see him standing there. Stopping him from making love to her the night before had been one of the hardest things she'd ever done, and for most of the night, she'd agonized over her decision.

It was obvious that he wanted her, and *damn*, she wanted him too. Having him practically toss her on the bathroom floor had shocked her, but it had also inflamed her blood until it had burned hot inside of her. She'd been so long without him—the only man she'd ever loved—that she didn't want to think about what was right or wrong. She just wanted him inside of her. Wanted it desperately.

Marlie had come apart almost the very moment he'd touched her, the pleasure only intensifying her need. But now that Rogan had gone to investigate the scream Wade had heard, she felt a chill crawl up her skin. Had something happened to Kevin?

Glancing at the clock on the mantel, Marlie saw that it was 9:05 a.m. She couldn't help but pace in front of the fireplace, clasping her hands together as her body trembled. Suddenly, there was a sharp knock on the door. Was that Rogan? Why didn't he just walk in? Marlie crossed the room to the door and opened it, only to gasp at the strange man on the other side.

"Please, can you help me?" he said, holding up his blood-covered hands.

Marlie couldn't help but suck in her breath. "Are you all right?"

"I had a car accident up the road. Do you have a phone I could use?"

Swallowing hard, Marlie stood there for a moment,

unsure of what to do. With a curt nod, she said, "Wait here; I'll get it for you."

Just as she stepped away from the open door, the man forced his way into the house and closed the door behind him. "That won't be necessary," he whispered into her ear as he grabbed her arm, twisting it up behind her.

"What are you doing?" she yelled, frightened and confused. Who the hell was this man she thought as she cried out with pain. Her mind was racing, and she hoped to God Rogan returned with her shotgun.

"Christ, you're covered in his stink," the man said, leading her into the kitchen. "How can you live with yourself?"

"What are you talking about?"

Marlie watched as the mysterious man turned on all four of the gas burners of the stove to high—then blew out the flames.

"What'd you do, sleep with him?" the man asked her in a gruff voice, yanking her back to the dining room table.

Marlie's heart was racing a mile a minute. What the hell did the man just turn on her gas stove for?

"Rogan!" she shouted but quickly paid for it as the man backhanded her right across the mouth. He had to have some kind of inhuman strength, because she flew across the room, seeing nothing but stars before her eyes as she hit the far wall. Her head was still swimming as he grabbed her roughly and sat her down on one of her dining room chairs. Tears filled her eyes, and she watched while he pulled a few lengths of rope from his jacket. He tied her wrists to the arms of the chair, only to be followed by her ankles.

"Please!" she cried as the tears poured onto her cheeks. "Please don't do this!"

"Sorry, my dear," the man said mockingly as he stood and wandered over to her fireplace. "Nothing personal, you understand. I just want to make that husband of yours suffer a bit. Losing you right after he found you again is sure to do the trick."

Understanding dawned on Marlie's face as he built a fire in the hearth. "You don't have to do this!" she screamed, trying to get herself free.

"Oh, but I do," the man said with a grin as he sauntered to the door. "Orders are orders." Grabbing the doorknob, he opened the door then turned to look back at her. "Better make your peace now, little lady. I think you have about… oh, thirty seconds to a minute before that gas makes its way to the fireplace. It was nice meeting you."

Marlie could feel the bile rising in the back of her throat. She realized with horror that the man was simply going to leave her there as he closed the door quietly behind him.

Seven

"Jesus!"

Rogan covered his nose and mouth with the sleeve of his shirt and tried his hardest to avoid puking on the ground in front of him. There, a few yards away, were the remains of Kevin, dragged from his vehicle and killed by some vicious creature.

"Shit," Rogan said through his teeth as he and Wade walked closer. A familiar scent assaulted his nostrils, and his blood ran cold. "Wade!" he exclaimed, glancing frantically down at the snow for evidence of what he was smelling.

"I know," Wade said, his eyes flashing. "I can smell that bastard too."

Rogan's hackles rose as he saw the footprints of a huge bear in the snow near Kevin's body. "Sean," he whispered.

"Where the hell did he go?" Wade asked, inhaling deeply as he weaved in and out of the surrounding trees.

With his skin crawling, Rogan cocked the shotgun in his hands and turned around, staring at Marlie's house a few hundred yards away.

"Christ, Wade! Marlie's alone!"

Rogan broke into a run.

~ * ~

The smell of natural gas surrounded Marlie as she tried her hardest to twist and turn against her bonds. Terror filled her heart at the knowledge that she was going to die. Now Rogan would have to live the rest of his life mourning *her*.

No! That was *not* going to happen!

Marlie realized the man had tied her to the broken chair—the one with the arm she'd been meaning to fix for the longest time. A ray of hope shot through her heart. With a sharp tug, she pulled her wrist upward, and the arm of the chair popped off the frame. It took her a moment to work her hand free from the rope, but once she did, she frantically began untying her other arm. When it was free as well, she grabbed her ankles with her shaking fingers, hoping to all that was holy that she'd have enough time to get out of the house before it blew.

It didn't take long before she was free, sprinting through the house and exiting out the rear door. She didn't want to risk that insane man seeing her flee the house by running out the front. Without stopping, she stumbled in the snow, crawling up the gentle slope of the hill behind her home. She had just enough time to jump behind a fallen tree as the massive explosion rocked the sky.

Marlie screamed and covered her head, terrified beyond reason as flaming bits of the house she'd lived in for years fell all around her.

~ * ~

Rogan and Wade both flew backward at the force of the blast. Thick plumes of smoke mushroomed into the sky, curling upwards as if reaching to Heaven.

"MARLIE!" Rogan screamed, trying to scramble to his feet.

Wade tackled him. "Rogan, don't! It's an inferno in

there!"

"I don't care! She's in there, Wade! I told her to stay put! Let me go!"

"No! She's gone, buddy. She's gone!"

"NO!"

Rogan wept as he crumbled to the ground, watching the house burn out of control. Rage boiled inside of him. He'd lost her—just when he'd found her again. Shit, he should have made love to her last night! Fat tears rolled down his cheeks as he hit the snow with his fists over and over in his anger.

"*AAAAAHHHH!*" Rogan was back on his feet, grabbing the shotgun and wiping his eyes.

"What are you doing?" Wade asked, his eyes wide.

"I'm going to kill that son of a bitch!"

"With a *shotgun*? Are you mad, Rogan? He's a Kodiak!"

"I don't give a shit!" Rogan's eyes flashed. "Let the bastard kill me too."

"You're upset, Rogan, but we've gotta go. I know she meant a lot to you, but she's gone. We have to go!"

"No, I won't leave her. *Not again!*"

"Marlie's dead!" Wade shouted.

Rogan balled his fist and punched him square in the jaw. Just as Wade went down, Rogan stepped over him and ran toward the burning remains of the house he'd bought with his wife, the gun firmly clutched in his hand.

~ * ~

Sean watched with glee as the house burned on its foundations. It was a beautiful sight to behold. Even from where he was a few hundred yards away, he could hear Rogan's screams of terror and anger at losing his wife. Sean chuckled to himself.

"Serves you right, you bastard," he muttered as he fingered the angry scar on his face that ran from his forehead to his chin, the scar Rogan had given him. Not more than a year ago, the scientists at B*E*A*S*T* had pitted him against Rogan in a fight to see which one of them would be the victor—the wolf or the grizzly.

They'd each fought for their lives, and neither of them had come out of the fight unscathed. Sean had never forgiven Rogan for giving him the scar he now bore, and it hadn't taken long before that anger had burned to hatred inside of him. The other shifters at B*E*A*S*T* had liked to taunt him, wondering how a mighty grizzly could have possibly been beaten by a mere timber wolf.

Yet he *hadn't* been beaten. The scientists had stopped the fight before there had been a victor, but it hadn't mattered. His inability to defeat Rogan Wolfe in a fair fight had been known far and wide throughout the B*E*A*S*T* compound, and Sean had never lived it down. He'd kill that damned wolf if it was the last thing he ever did.

A familiar flowery scent assaulted his nostrils, and his anger flared anew. Shit! The woman had escaped the explosion!

No matter. She would die today; he'd make sure of it. The woman had no hope against him. No hope at all.

With a growl, Sean stripped once again there in the snow and shifted.

Eight

As Rogan charged the house with tears in his eyes, a wonderful scent wafted to him on the breeze. Something familiar, tugging on his memory. He stopped for a moment while he breathed deeply, trying hard not to cough as the acrid smoke burned his lungs. Every hair on his body stood on end as he recognized the scent.

Marlie!

Following the faint flowery scent, he rounded the house near a small rise, swallowing his thundering heart.

"Oh, please, *please* let her be alive!" he cried, not even sure who he was speaking to. He didn't dare get too close to the burning house, which was now setting a few of the surrounding trees on fire. But as he approached the small hill, Marlie's scent became much more pronounced.

"Marlie!" he called, trudging through the snow. "*Marlie!*"

"Rogan!"

His eyes followed the sound of her voice to the top of the hill and saw his wife crouched behind a fallen tree. Rogan ran up the gentle slope and jumped over the log, dropping the gun at the same time. Instantly his arms went around her as he cried into her neck, holding her close, crushing her to him. He inhaled deeply, threading his fingers through her hair, pulling away just enough to kiss her lips. Again and again he kissed her, relief flowing through him like a rushing wind.

"Shit, Marlie! I thought you were dead," he said, sniffling and gazing into her eyes. She was crying too, the trail of her tears clearly evident on her face.

"I thought I was too."

Once again he wrapped his arms around her, clinging to her with all of his might. She was the last link he had to his life before. He could *not* lose her. Not now, not ever.

"Don't let go of me," she said into his ear.

Rogan caressed her trembling shoulders and whispered, "I won't, sweetheart. I'm not ever going to leave you again."

With his words, she clutched him even tighter. A roar rocked the trees at that moment, making Rogan's breathing stop.

"What the hell was that?" Marlie asked, glancing around with frightened eyes.

"We've got to go," Rogan said, grabbing the shotgun off the ground.

"What is that, Rogan?"

"No time to explain, honey. Let's just go!"

Another roar lifted into the air behind them, closer this time. Rogan leapt over the log once more and lifted Marlie over it as well. Looking over her shoulder, he could see Sean—in his grizzly state—charging them through the trees. He was more massive than Rogan remembered, and a sudden terror gripped him. Rogan could shift and easily get away from the lumbering bear, but Marlie couldn't.

"Marlie, run!" he yelled, pushing her down the slope of the hill.

"But, Rogan—"

"Do it, damn it!"

Rogan aimed the gun and fired. He had no idea if Marlie had heeded his words as he cocked the gun and aimed once more. He could hear the bear's heavy breathing as it charged, getting closer by the second. Rogan knew he must have hit Sean with that first shot, but it had done nothing to bring him down.

Rogan fired the gun again, and Sean stumbled in the snow, sliding to a stop. He was growling and snarling, clawing at his face. Rogan didn't allow himself to feel elated. All he'd done was piss the grizzly off. Taking that moment to flee, he turned and ran down the hill, relieved that Marlie had done as he'd said. She was running a few yards in front of him, and it didn't take long before he'd caught up with her. He grabbed her elbow and helped her along.

Another roar rose from the trees behind them, and Rogan cursed foully. The sound of an engine suddenly drifted to his ears and within mere moments, a yellow Hummer crashed through the foliage with Wade at the wheel. They'd hidden the truck near the main road and walked the rest of the way to stake out Marlie's house the day before. Thank God Wade had enough common sense to go get the damn thing and enough empathy to forgive Rogan for punching his lights out. He'd apologize for that later.

The Hummer braked hard, coming to a stop yet still rocking from the force of it. Without hesitation, Rogan ripped open the passenger door and hoisted Marlie into the truck. Wade grabbed her arm and helped her climb into the back. As soon as she was in, Rogan jumped into the seat and slammed the door shut behind him.

"Go, go, *go!*" he yelled, his eyes wide as he glanced through the windshield. There was Sean, only a few yards away, bloody and charging the Hummer.

Wade slammed into reverse, and the truck lurched as

he looked over his shoulder.

"Can't this piece of shit go any faster?" Rogan exclaimed.

"You wanna drive?" Wade growled, his face set in stone.

"He's still coming, Wade. Jesus!"

"What the hell is going on?" Marlie cried from the back.

Rogan ignored her for the time being and reloaded the shotgun with the shells he'd stuffed in his pocket from Marlie's kitchen. After rolling down the window, he pointed the gun and fired, but it did nothing to stop Sean.

"You're wasting the shot!" Wade said with irritation. "Have a little faith!"

With that, the truck hit a bump, and all three of them jumped at the impact. Finally, they had a paved road under their wheels. Wade pulled out onto the road, jammed the Hummer into drive, and slammed on the accelerator. The tires were slick from the snow and squealed on the road, just as Sean broke through the trees. Before the Hummer could get its grip on the road, the giant bear slammed his head into the driver's side door.

"CHRIST!" Wade yelled, holding up his arms while Marlie screamed at the top of her lungs.

But before Sean could do any more damage, the truck's wheels found their purchase, and they sped off down the road. Rogan frantically looked out the back window only to see Sean unable to keep up behind them. They were losing him. Laying his head back on the seat, Rogan sighed with relief.

"Holy *shit*, Wolfe," Wade said, running his shaking hand through his hair. "My entire life flashed before my eyes! Granted, it was only like two years, but…"

Rogan chuckled. Wiping his eyes, he took in deep gulps of air. "God, mine did too. Mine *and* hers."

Glancing over his shoulder, Rogan saw Marlie curled up into a ball on the floor of the truck. There was no back seat, just cheap carpet and a few compartments along the side walls full of changes of clothes, first-aid kits, and vials of serum—the shit that prevented a shifter from changing from one form to another no matter what state he was in for at least four hours. Rogan shuddered, remembering the times when he'd been trapped in his animal form after being forced to take the serum back in the labs at the B*E*A*S*T* compound.

But he refused to think about that. Right now, he needed to comfort his wife.

Nine

“Marlie? Marlie, are you all right?”

Her body trembled violently, and she covered her head with her hands. Something touched her and she squealed. Her frantic eyes glanced around the cab to see Rogan kneeling over her. With a cry of relief, she sat up and flung herself into his arms. Unable to hold back any longer, Marlie sobbed into his shoulder. She tried to talk, but all that came out was more sobbing. It was hard to draw breath as she hugged him, refusing to let go of him for even a moment.

“It’s all right,” he murmured in her ear. “It’s all right, sweetheart. We’re safe.”

“Rogan—”

“Shh,” he said, covering her lips with his finger. “Just let me hold you for awhile before you talk.”

Marlie nodded, turning her face into his neck. His familiar scent eventually calmed her, and the heat from his body seeped into her skin. After a few minutes, her crying was reduced to mere sniffles.

“What’s going on?” she asked in a small voice.

Rogan pulled back just enough to look into her face.

He tucked her hair behind her ears and wiped the tears away with the pads of his thumbs.

"B*E*A*S*T* has found us."

Marlie's eyes widened. "What do you mean? Who was that man, Rogan? And where the hell did that bear come from?"

Rogan took a deep breath and sighed. Sitting down on the floor of the Hummer, he pulled Marlie across his lap. "Remember when Wade told you we'd freed the shifters back at the B*E*A*S*T* compound?"

"Yes," she said, biting her lower lip.

"Well, that kinda put us on B*E*A*S*T*'s most wanted list. They want to kill us."

Marlie gasped as more tears filled her eyes.

"There is a man at B*E*A*S*T* named Sean Ross who hates me. He's a shifter, just like me and Wade."

"A… a…" Marlie couldn't even bring herself to say it. A chill ran down her spine as she stared into her husband's eyes. They flashed at her for just a moment—a bright gold color. Marlie gasped, and Rogan's grip on her waist tightened.

"Yes," he said. "A shifter."

Closing her eyes, Marlie tried hard to ignore her pounding heart. Could Rogan hear it with his keen ears? She had no idea, but he had to smell her fear. Looking back at him, she saw his eyes soften just as he raised his hand to stroke her face.

"He was the bear we saw, Marlie."

"Oh my God, Rogan," she said as her tears fell again. "That man cuh-came to the duh-door. He… tied me up to the chair and turned on the gas. I thought I was going to… to die." Clutching onto his neck, she could feel his body shudder.

"I thought you *had* died," he whispered into her ear. His voice cracked. "When I saw the house blow, I thought you were inside."

"Oh, Matthew, our house!" Once again, she began wailing.

"Rogan," he corrected softly, caressing her hair.

"Where are we going to... where am *I* going to live?"

Rogan was silent for so long that she leaned back and looked at him.

"Right now, your home is this Hummer. With me."

"My family—"

"No."

"*Your* family—"

"No! Marlie, B*E*A*S*T* would kill them. Those bastards have no remorse, no qualms about taking the lives of innocent people. We're on our own here."

"But your mother, Rogan. She deserves to know you're alive."

"My mother mourns her son *Matthew*, who died two years ago. I'm a different man, Marlie. I'm changed. I can't go back to that life and pretend like none of this ever happened!"

"You came back to *me*." Holding his eye contact was one of the hardest things she'd ever done.

Rogan licked his lips. "Only because you are the one thing I can remember from my life before. I had to know if what I was remembering was real or a dream. And you had the right to know that you weren't a widow after all."

"But I *am* a widow," she whispered, playing with the top button on his shirt. "You said yourself that Matthew Silver is dead. According to the state, all the paperwork has been filed. If you have no intention of becoming that man again, then... we're not married anymore."

He looked as if she'd just punched him in the gut. "Do you believe that?"

His voice was low and soft, but she could tell by the

set of his shoulders that his body was tense, waiting for her answer. Long moments of silence passed between them before she could reply.

"No. Marriage is more than a piece of paper for me. It's a promise to be with one person until the day they die. I thought you were dead, but you're not. My promise to you as your wife still stands in my eyes."

Rogan closed his eyes and bowed his head as if relieved. He glanced at her once more. "You said your promise lasts until the day your husband dies. Did you… Marlie, when you found out I was dead, did you…"

"What?" she asked when he let the sentence hang.

"Were you… *with* anyone after I was gone?"

Marlie stared at him a moment before understanding dawned on her. She sucked in her breath. He wanted to know if she'd slept with anyone after his death.

Stroking his face, she kissed his cheek. "No," she whispered into his ear before kissing his mouth, then his other cheek. "I was faithful. After holding Heaven in my arms, how could I possibly settle for anything less?"

Rogan groaned at her words but didn't speak. He grabbed her face and kissed her without reserve. His tongue demanded entry into her mouth, boldly staking its claim on hers. Marlie kissed him back with fervor, once again rejoicing that she was in his arms. All the tears she'd cried over his death and all the lonely nights were forgotten as her palms slid along his cheeks into his hair.

She couldn't get close enough.

She scooted on his lap, trying to press herself against him, but the way her legs sprawled across his made it almost impossible. Rogan growled low in his throat.

"This is not the time or the place for this," he whispered as he pulled away, taking deep breaths along her throat, as if inhaling her essence.

Shivers raced down Marlie's spine.

"I love the smell of your desire, woman," he said, his voice gritty and low.

The tips of Rogan's fingers gently grazed her nipple, making it pucker. She would have begged for more of his touch if Wade hadn't been in the car with them, and the fire in Rogan's eyes told her he would have continued. Covering his hand with hers, she held it to her breast and leaned back onto his shoulder as he cupped her, listening to his heartbeat while he traced lazy circles on her through her clothing. After a few minutes of basking in his embrace, Marlie had a thought.

"Rogan?"

"Hmm?" he asked, leaning his head against hers.

"That scream outside… was it that Sean guy?"

Rogan took a deep breath. "No, Sean didn't scream."

"Then who was it?"

"You don't want to know."

Marlie sat up and scowled at him. "Damn it, Rogan, I *do* want to know! My house was just blown to kingdom come. I deserve to know who the hell was screaming outside."

Running his fingers through his hair, Rogan sighed. "It was Kevin."

"Oh my God, he was *out* there? Did you help him? Did he run into the bear?" Marlie's eyes once again filled with tears, dreading his answer.

"Marlie, Kevin's dead."

Gasping into her hand, Marlie stared at Rogan in horror as he said his next words.

"Sean killed him."

"He's dead?" she repeated, not wanting to believe it.

Rogan nodded, his eyes filled with sympathy. "I'm sorry, sweetheart. But he's gone."

Marlie paled, and she felt as if she were going to be sick.

"Are you all right?" Rogan asked.

Laying her head on his shoulder, she shuddered. "After today, I don't think I'll ever be all right again."

He pulled her closer to his chest. Nothing more was said as he stroked her hair. The miles passed in silence.

Ten

Sean was bleeding. Bleeding badly. He grunted as he pulled on the clothing he'd left in the snow before shifting to chase after Rogan and Marlie. The bastard had shot him. That goddamn wolf had once again gotten the better of him!

His skin was now pockmarked with holes, the many pellets he'd been shot with embedded inside of him. The pain only served to make his anger burn hotter than it ever had before. Rogan was going to *pay* for this.

Breathing through his gritted teeth, Sean zipped his pants and grabbed his jacket off the ground, and the side pocket began to ring. Digging into it, he pulled out his cell phone and flipped it open.

"Ross here," he said curtly, blinking hard to clear the cloud of pain from his eyes.

"Report."

Shit. It was Covington.

"They got away."

Silence greeted his words, then: "I'm not in the mood for your games." Clive Covington always had been an asshole.

"I'm not playing with you," Sean said.

“You damn well better be!” Clive yelled. “I sent you to Alaska to kill Rogan Wolfe, not let him get away!”

Sean’s vision turned red with rage. “My plan backfired.”

“That much is obvious!”

“It’s not a total bust, sir,” Sean said, trying hard to remain civil with the man who funded the B*E*A*S*T* agency.

“Do tell,” Clive said, his voice dripping with sarcasm.

Sean growled to himself. “I planted a GPS locator beacon on Rogan’s Hummer. I’ll be able to find him.”

“You’d better hope you do,” Clive said in a softly menacing voice. “I own you, Mr. Ross. And I’m not afraid of you. The next time we talk, I want to hear results, not failures.”

“Yes sir,” Sean said, biting his lip to keep from crying out in pain and frustration as he walked to his own vehicle hidden amongst the trees near the main road. Without waiting to see if the wealthy benefactor had anything more to say, Sean snapped his phone shut and muttered under his breath, “Bastard.”

Just because Clive had money in the bank, he thought he held all the cards. Truth be told, it was the *shifters* who had all the real power. If it weren’t for the men who were still loyal to B*E*A*S*T*, the agency wouldn’t be able to function.

Clive Covington needed to be taught a lesson, but not before Sean killed Rogan. He’d fulfill his mission as promised, *then* he’d make his way back to Texas to have a few choice words with the senator.

Sean had to smile as he crawled into the driver’s seat of his own B*E*A*S*T* issued black Hummer. So Clive wasn’t afraid of him, huh? One of these days, he’d endeavor to change Covington’s mind about that.

His belly growled at the thought.

Eleven

"Does anyone know where the hell we are?" Wade's voice broke through the silence in the truck.

Marlie felt drained. She could barely lift her head off Rogan's shoulder. She knew his body must be screaming from sitting in one position for so long—and with her sprawled across his lap, no less—but he hadn't complained. Marlie liked listening to his heartbeat, slow and steady and a comforting reminder that he wasn't dead. He was alive and well—and holding her in his arms.

"About five more miles and we'll reach a junction with Glenn Highway," she answered Wade. "Go south, and we'll head straight to Anchorage."

Closing her eyes, Marlie bit the inside of her lip. What was she going to do now? Everything she'd owned had been blown to bits right before her eyes. A shiver raced through her veins at the memory. Rogan stirred but didn't move her off his lap.

"What's to the north?" Wade asked, squinting at the glare of the sunlight reflecting off the snow outside.

Marlie yawned before answering. "A whole lotta mountains."

"What do you think, Wolfe? North or south?"

Rogan took a deep breath before he spoke. "We'll need to make it to some kind of civilization to eat."

"There are a few lodges and small towns up north," Marlie said.

"True," Rogan countered. "But Anchorage has an airport."

"What are you thinking?" Wade asked.

"Sean has found us. He'll keep coming for us unless we get the hell out of Dodge. I say we call up Noah and see if we can hole up with him for awhile."

"Your friend Noah?" Marlie asked. When Rogan nodded, she said, "But how are you going to call him? Isn't he moving from place to place like you said?"

"Well, yeah," Rogan said. "But before we left Colorado, we all bought disposable cell phones so we could call each other whenever we want without the fear of B*E*A*S*T* tracing our calls."

Marlie stared at him for a moment, taking in his words. "But you want to leave Alaska?"

"Why not? We don't have anything to stay for."

Marlie knew he was right. Aside from her job at the tiny vet clinic in Rivers Fork, she had nothing holding her to the region. Still, she had to ask him about it.

"What about my job?"

"Sean found your home. I think it's a safe bet to say he also knows where you work. Marlie, he tried to kill you. He'll try again and again until he succeeds. He's not going to stop."

"But why? Why does he want *me* dead? What have *I* ever done to him?"

"You're my wife. That's all the justification he needs."

"My God. The man must be insane!"

"Pretty damn close," Wade said from the driver's seat. "Sometimes I wonder if any of us are sane."

When Marlie's eyes touched Rogan's once more, she held her breath. Was Rogan unstable? Whatever those assholes at the agency had done to him, they'd mutated his genetic code. It was entirely possible that he didn't have all the lights on upstairs.

"Why are you looking at me like that?" he asked, breaking her out of her own morbid thoughts.

"Like what?" she asked, unsure about revealing her doubts to him.

"Like I just grew a third eye," he said sarcastically, lifting his mouth in a half-grin. "I might be able to change my shape at will, but as far as I know, wolves only have two eyes just like people."

Marlie blushed and looked away. "I was just wondering if you two were… a little nutty yourselves."

"Isn't it obvious?" Wade said with a grin, glancing at them in the rear-view mirror. Marlie couldn't help but chuckle.

"We're not crazy, if that's what you mean," Rogan said, finally shifting his weight to get a better seat on the floor. "Wade might get a few hair-brained ideas, but I wouldn't say he's ready for his own padded cell. Yet."

Wade scoffed. "I've been in enough cells to last me a lifetime, thank you very much."

Marlie gasped. "You were put into cells?"

"Oh, yeah." Rogan nodded. "There were hundreds of us, all kept in cages. They tested us in groups, which is how I became such good friends with Noah and Wade."

"Don't forget Justin." Wade's voice drifted through the cab, and an oppressive silence followed his words.

"I have *not* forgotten Justin," Rogan whispered, his voice deep and gritty.

"Who's Justin?" Marlie asked, stroking his cheek. Rogan was somewhere else just then, as if remembering something from the past.

"He was a good friend of mine. A good friend to all of us."

"What happened to him?"

Rogan swallowed hard and glanced out the rear window of the truck. "He was killed. By Sean."

"Dear God! Does that man kill everyone in his path?"

"You don't know the half of it," Rogan said, gently tucking a stray lock of her hair behind her ear. "That bastard has another thing coming if he thinks he can get the best of Rogan Wolfe."

Marlie sucked in her breath as his eyes flashed, sending a bolt of fear straight up her spine and goose bumps down her arms and legs. "Please don't get yourself killed," she whispered to him. "I wouldn't be able to survive if I lost you again."

"Don't you worry, sweetheart," he said, framing her face in his hands. "I don't intend to be killed. I intend to be the one doing the killing."

Marlie didn't know which would be harder to bear—losing her husband a second time to death, or losing him to revenge. With that thought, she wrapped her arms around his waist and held on tightly, hoping for the best, yet fearing the worst.

~ * ~

Once they'd reached the junction to Glenn Highway, they turned south. Wade drove until they came to a small gas station where they filled up the tank and stocked up on food from the small convenience store.

"I'm starving," Marlie said as she accepted a package of powered donuts and a bottle of Diet Coke.

"Me too," Rogan said, practically drooling as he

unwrapped a small tuna sandwich. He ate half the sandwich in two bites.

"I could eat an entire moose," Wade said as he climbed into the passenger seat since it was Rogan's turn to drive. "I could probably take one down if we get desperate."

"That's not funny," Rogan said, cocking a brow at his friend.

Wade gave him a wounded look. "Well, Marlie's smiling."

Marlie had to bite her lip to keep from giggling at their banter.

"She's only smiling because she's eating yummy pastries."

"Oh, is that so?"

"It is," Rogan said, his mouth full of the rest of his sandwich.

Wade turned to her and winked, moaning as he bit into his apple turnover. "Thiff iff the beft appol turmovuh I've eva hab."

"Good Lord, Wade," Rogan said with a scoff. "Don't talk with your mouth full. It's disgusting." He turned the key and pulled the truck back onto the highway.

"You just did it," Wade protested, peeling back the wrapping and taking another large bite.

Rogan rolled his eyes. "Do you even remember ever eating another apple turnover you can compare this one with?"

Wade swallowed hard. "No. Which is why this is the best one I've ever had!"

Marlie couldn't help but chuckle. After the terrifying morning they'd had, a little levity was exactly what she needed. It was already getting late in the afternoon, and they still had a long way to go. They wouldn't make it to Anchorage before nightfall. "Tired?"

Marlie looked up and saw Rogan glancing at her in

the rearview mirror.

She nodded with a yawn. “Yeah. How’d you know?”

“I can smell it.”

She blinked, still not used to his new abilities.

“Why don’t you pull out some pillows and a blanket?” Rogan said. “Get some rest.”

“I’m not sure I can,” she replied truthfully, running her fingers through her hair.

“Why don’t you try? You’re safe now.”

He was right. And the thought of lying back and escaping into sleep did sound inviting. Rummaging through the storage containers along the walls of the truck, Marlie found what she needed amidst the clothes, first aid supplies, and water bottles. With a deep sigh, she curled up on the floor, and before she knew it, she was sound asleep.

Twelve

"Shit!"

Rogan's heart was in his throat as he felt the Hummer suddenly shudder, losing power despite his foot on the gas pedal. Wisps of white smoke wafted from underneath the hood, and Rogan glanced at Wade.

"This can't be good," Wade said, chewing the inside of his lip.

Rogan growled. "Don't do this now, damn it!" He pulled the truck over to the side of the road. It rolled to a stop and stalled.

"Definitely not good," Wade muttered.

Marlie sat up in the back and asked sleepily, "What's going on?"

Rogan gripped the steering wheel tightly before slamming open the driver's side door. "The damn truck just broke down!"

He pulled on the lever under the dash that popped open the hood. Without waiting to hear if she had anything more to say, Rogan jumped out of the Hummer and yanked the hood up over his head.

"Know anything about cars?" Wade asked, rounding

the vehicle next to him and glancing at the steaming engine.

Rogan gave him a sour look. "What do you think?"

Wade shrugged. "It was worth asking."

"Damn it." Rogan watched as the smoke drifted up. He could feel the heat coming off the transmission. "I think we forgot to put anti-freeze in it."

"We just filled it with water back in Canada," Wade said, pointing over his shoulder with his thumb.

"I said *anti-freeze.*" Rogan sighed. "It's damn cold here in Alaska."

Wade's eyes widened. "You think the water froze in there and the engine overheated?"

"Probably."

"Can you fix it?" Marlie's voice floated in the air, and her scent suddenly hit Rogan full force. She was concerned but a little frightened as well. It was all he could do to keep from pulling her into his arms.

"I don't think so," he said, casting her a glance.

"Then what are we going to do?"

Rogan looked at Wade, then back at Marlie. "We'll have to hoof it, I guess."

"You mean walk?" she exclaimed.

"We can't just sit here, Marlie," Rogan said, closing the hood.

"But I don't even have a jacket, and it's freezing out here."

Wade shrugged out of the coat he was wearing and handed it to her. "I'm sorry," he said sheepishly. "I don't know where my manners have gone."

"What about you?" she asked.

"I'll be fine. I think we're all a little immune to the cold."

Rogan watched as his wife donned the jacket, lamenting that Wade's scent would now be on her skin. He knew his friend didn't have any inclination of getting closer to Marlie, but he still didn't like the thought of another man's scent on his mate.

"How far is it to Anchorage?" Rogan asked, just to keep his mind occupied.

"I don't know," Marlie replied. "Maybe another thirty miles."

"Damn."

"We could flag down some motorist," Wade suggested. "Hitch a ride into town."

Rogan shook his head. "No."

"But—"

"No! Remember what Tam did to the poor man Noah and Lanie hitched a ride with? If Sean catches anyone who helped us, he'll kill them too. I'm not going to risk anyone's life like that."

An uncomfortable silence descended upon them. Rogan could see Marlie shivering even underneath the warm jacket.

"Come on," he said as he draped his arm around her shoulders. "Let's see what we can salvage from the truck and be on our way."

He grabbed a couple packages of beef jerky, a few bottles of water, and the syringes of serum. Holding the stuff made him bite his lip to keep from growling. If he had his way, he'd dump it all right here on the side of the road, but they were being pursued by Sean—it would be stupid not to take it. He stuffed the syringes into his back pocket. Glancing down at Marlie's shotgun on the floor of the cab, he grabbed that too.

Wade clutched a few blankets and changes of clothing while Marlie took the shopping bag of the food they'd purchased from the convenience store.

"Can't forget this," Rogan said, opening the glove box. Inside was a stack of twenty dollar bills that he quickly stuffed into his pockets as well.

"Where did you get that?" Marlie asked with a gasp, peering over his shoulder.

"We stole more than this Hummer from B*E*A*S*T*," Rogan said. Underneath the money were two cell phones. Rogan pocketed one while handing the other to Wade. "All right then. Do we have everything we need?"

"I think so," Wade said. "You really think we can walk all the way to Anchorage in this weather?"

"We're gonna have to." Rogan pulled out his phone and sighed. "Can't get good cell coverage up here. If we're going to call Noah, we'll have to get closer to the city."

At that moment, a car could be heard approaching them from the way they came.

"Get off the road," Rogan said, grabbing the collar of Marlie's jacket. "We don't want them to see us and stop to offer a ride."

All three of them slinked into the tree line on the side of the highway. As the car approached, they could tell it was another Hummer, black and pristine.

"Oh my God," Wade whispered, watching in shock as the second Hummer pulled up behind their yellow one. "That's Sean!"

"We gotta run. *Now!*" Rogan grabbed Marlie's arm and pulled her through the trees with Wade following close behind.

~ * ~

The instant Sean opened his car door, a wall of stench assaulted his nostrils. He grimaced, yet he still had to smile to himself. Those bastards hadn't gotten far. Not only had he tagged Rogan's Hummer with a GPS locator beacon, he'd also drained the radiator. If he hadn't been in so much pain, Sean would have chuckled with delight.

He heard a crash in the bushes to his right and caught a glimpse of the traitors fleeing through the woods as fast as their feet could carry them. Limping to the back of his truck, Sean opened one of the rear doors. He knew he wouldn't be able to catch them, not wounded as he was. Fortunately, he had a tranquilizer gun in the back full of darts tipped with B*E*A*S*T*'s serum. Those bastards had another thing coming if they thought they could get away so easily.

Hissing through his teeth, Sean trudged back to the hood of his car, loading the weapon as he walked. Leaning on the hood, he took careful aim—and fired.

~ * ~

Son of a bitch! How did Sean find us?

Rogan's thoughts raced, but he didn't dare take the time to stop and wonder about that now. They needed to get away, and fast.

Suddenly the sound of a gun blast filled the air, then Wade hit the ground hard.

"Wade!" Rogan stopped running and fell to his knees beside his friend. "Are you all right?" He saw the tranquilizer dart sticking out of Wade's back. "Shit!"

"Rogan, get out of here," Wade panted. "Get your wife to safety."

"But you're shot!"

"Don't worry about me. Just go."

"That bastard killed Justin. He'll kill you too, Wade! I'm not leaving you!"

"If he wanted me dead, he would have shot me with a bullet, not a tranquilizer. Christ…" Wade's voice was getting softer. "I think he shot me with the serum too. Can't… shift…"

"Wade? *Wade!*" Rogan was frantic. He dropped the gun and grabbed both of Wade's hands, trying to pull him to his feet although he knew it would be hopeless to outrun Sean if he had to drag Wade.

"Get… out of here," Wade said, closing his eyes.

"I'll be… all right. Go."

With tears in his eyes, Rogan let go of Wade and grabbed Marlie instead, scooping up the shotgun once more. "I'm sorry, old buddy," he said, sniffling. "I'm so sorry!"

"Wait. Rogan, *wait!*" Marlie protested.

"Don't look back," Rogan said, once again sprinting through the trees with her in tow. "Whatever you do, sweetheart. Don't look back!"

~ * ~

Tears ran down Marlie's face as they ran. She could hear two more gunshots behind them but they must have gone wide. Rogan pulled her along by her left hand, and she lamented that she had dropped the bag of food in their haste to get away. But the thought of that horrid man chasing them again spurned her on, even after her lungs caught fire.

Memories of the bear charging them near her house that morning ripped through her head, and it was all she could do to keep up with Rogan. Hot tears blurred her vision, making it nearly impossible to see. But after a few minutes of running at full bore, Rogan stopped and smiled.

"Perfect."

In front of them was a large creek rushing over rocks and stones. The other side was at least ten yards away. She didn't understand why Rogan was smiling and didn't have the breath to ask him. Before she could gulp enough air to form the words, he'd dragged her into the frigid waters.

Thirteen

Sean flipped open his phone as he walked toward the still form of the man lying face down in the snow. He grimaced when he saw only one bar on the LCD screen. He'd be lucky if the call even connected. Punching a few buttons, he glanced up at the sky before hunkering down next to Wade, whose eyes were now glassed over. As the phone rang in his ear, it crackled in and out.

"Damn, the reception is shitty up here," Sean said aloud.

"Covington," came the distant voice on the other end.

"I've got one of them," Sean said, pushing on Wade's shoulder just to make sure he was indeed tranquilized.

"Rogan?"

"No. The other one."

Covington was silent for a moment. "Wade?"

"That's the one."

"Don't harm him," Covington said, clearing his throat. "I want him alive."

"What the hell am I supposed to do with him?" Sean

tossed his hands up in exasperation.

"Oh, I don't know. Let's see..." Clive retorted. "Why don't you reminisce about old times?"

Sean growled.

"Do I have to spell it out for you, Sean? Go to Anchorage. Find Brett. He'll bring the cougar back to Texas."

"By the time I get back to hunting Rogan, the trail will be cold!"

"What about the GPS beacon you planted?"

"Worked like a charm. Unfortunately, when I found their truck, I also found the traitors fleeing into the woods."

"Jesus Chr... can't you do anything right?"

"You want this cougar, old man?" Sean snapped, pissed at Covington's attitude. "You send Brett to *me*. There's a locator beacon on my truck too. He can find me just as easily. Right now, I've got a wolf to hunt."

With that, Sean snapped the phone shut and stuffed it into the pocket of his jeans.

"Here kitty, kitty," he said under his breath as he hoisted Wade up and over his shoulders. Christ, the bastard was heavy.

Sean puffed with exertion as he trudged through the snow back to the road. There was no way in hell he was going to let Rogan's trail grow cold. Not when he was so close to killing the prick.

~ * ~

Marlie gasped, almost unable to breathe the moment the icy waters came in contact with the skin of her legs. This water was one hundred percent melted snow—so cold, in fact, that Marlie really had no idea why it wasn't frozen over.

"Ruh-Ro... guh-gan!" she said, gasping between syllables. "Wuh-wait!"

He ran a few more steps before stopping abruptly to

spin around and look at her. “Shit!” he exclaimed, right before he lifted her in his arms. “Christ, Marlie. I’m sorry. I wasn’t thinking!”

Rogan walked upstream a bit before crossing to the far side of the creek. Once there, he bounded into the trees as if he hadn’t just been submerged thigh-deep into ice-cold water. After a few more minutes of running, he slowed then turned around to stop and listen.

“Shh,” he whispered to her as he glanced behind them, taking deep breaths of air. “There are wolves nearby,” he said, grinning to himself.

“Huh-how cuh-cuh-close?”

Rogan looked sharply at her and grimaced. “Are you all right?”

Marlie shook her head violently, unable to stop her body’s fierce trembling. “Suh-so cuh-cold…” she managed to say through chattering teeth.

“Damn. Your lips are turning blue! I should have known better than to drag you into that water.”

“Why?” she asked, clutching onto him with a vengeance. “Why duh-duh-did yuh-you?”

Rogan began walking again, still carrying Marlie in his arms. “To hide our scent. It won’t get rid of it completely, but it will buy us some time. Sean will have to search the riverbanks before he finds it again, and he’ll be gambling as to which way we went, upstream or down. And there are wolves nearby. That’s a good thing.”

Marlie’s teeth chattered so loud that she thought they might rattle right out of her head. “Oh?”

“Yeah,” he answered, quickening his pace. “The wolves will confuse him. Since we are a genetic match to the creatures we shift into, our scent isn’t that much different from the real deal.”

After a few moments, Marlie asked, “Are-aren’t you cuh-cold?”

"The water was cold, yes. But I'm not as affected by it as you. We need to get you someplace warm. Wade's jacket isn't going to be enough to ward off hypothermia."

"Just duh-don't luh-leave me," she said.

"Never again, woman." Rogan's words came from low in his throat.

Marlie couldn't help but smile at that. "Yuh-you always were a guh-good man," she told him.

"Not anymore," he said dryly, climbing a small rise.

"You still are."

"Only in *your* eyes."

"I'm the only wuh-one who muh-matters," she said, smiling as he met her gaze.

Nothing more was said as he gave her a squeeze, telling her without words that she was right.

~ * ~

It was dusk. The sun had just set when Rogan saw a structure through the trees not too far away. Was that a house? He couldn't be sure. The cold was finally getting to him. Both he and Marlie needed to warm up—and soon. Marlie was shaking so badly that it was all he could do to keep a grip on her.

"Hold on, honey," he whispered as he cleared the tree line.

It *was* a house! It seemed as if he'd stumbled upon a small community nestled amidst the trees, away from the main highway.

Slinking toward the houses, Rogan was drawn to a dark one not too far away. He kept in the shadows as well as he could and grinned from ear to ear when he saw his salvation: a *For Sale* sign.

This house was empty.

Rogan rounded the house to the back yard and rejoiced when he saw that the rear doors to the home were window-paned French doors.

"Can you stand, Marlie?" he asked.

Her face had been pressed into his shoulder. She licked her lips but nodded slowly.

"Only for a moment, sweetheart," he said. "I promise."

He set her gently on her feet before making sure she could indeed stand on her own. She stumbled against the wall of the house but was able to hold her own weight. Without wasting any time, Rogan took the butt of the shotgun and smashed one of the window panes in the door, right near the deadbolt. In mere moments, he'd unlocked the door and it swung wide open.

Rogan once again swept his wife into his arms before entering the house, closing the door behind him. Glancing around the dining room, he grinned. Whoever was selling this house hadn't completely moved out. There were still a few pieces of furniture here and there. Maybe he could find a blanket somewhere. He strode into the living room and set Marlie on the couch.

"Will you be all right?" he asked. "I'm going to go look for a blanket."

Her teeth continued to chatter as she lay there. "Yuh-yes," she answered. "Huh-hurry."

"I will," he said, leaning the gun against the wall.

He checked every closet on the main floor and cursed under his breath when he found nothing. *Damn it!* Racing up the stairs two at a time, he searched the linen closet in the hall.

"Bingo," he whispered. Folded neatly on the floor of the closet was a down comforter. Taking a deep breath, he could smell only the detergent used to wash it. The comforter was clean. Grabbing it in his arms, he raced back downstairs to Marlie.

"Come on, baby. Let's get you out of these wet clothes," he said, moving the coffee table out of the way as he sat her up on the couch. She didn't fight him while he stripped her out of her jacket and sweater. Even her delicate skin had a bluish cast to it.

He stopped for a moment when he noticed the necklace she wore. Her wedding ring was nestled between her breasts, winking at him in the dim light. A surge of possessiveness pulsed through him, and he had to bite his lip to keep from growling. She hadn't been wearing it when they'd showered together, which meant she must have put it on after their interlude on the bathroom floor that morning.

Rogan was suddenly overcome by the need to make her his once again. He yanked off his own shirt, telling himself that Marlie needed skin-to-skin contact to get warm. Hell, so did he.

"What are yuh-you duh-duh-doing?" she asked.

"We're getting undressed. Our clothes are wet and cold. We need our shared body heat if we're going to get warm."

Marlie tried to unfasten her jeans, but her fingers were too stiff to grab hold of the zipper. Pushing her hands away, Rogan did it himself, trying to ignore where his thoughts were headed. There was no time for *that*.

Marlie watched him as he yanked off her pants, followed by her panties. She still shivered from head to toe, but she gasped whenever his hands touched her. He had a feeling she was thinking exactly what he was.

Looking at her naked, he was reminded just how beautiful his wife truly was. On his knees before her, Rogan held her eye contact and unzipped his own jeans. There was no way to hide the effect her gaze had on him as he tugged his pants down over his hips, and he saw Marlie bite her lip as she looked at him.

Once he was as naked as she was, he held his hand out to her. He didn't say a word, but he could tell she knew what he wanted because she took his hand and scooted down to lie on the floor. Rogan lay down next to her and pulled the comforter over them both. When his arm pulled her close to his body, he could feel her shudder, and he shuddered too at the contact of her icy skin on his. But that didn't stop him from draping his leg over hers in an effort to press her even closer into his warmth.

The closer the better.

He just hoped he'd be able to forget about his lust for five friggin' minutes. But with Marlie wiggling her gloriously naked body against him, that wasn't bloody likely.

Fourteen

Marlie shivered and pressed closer, amazed at the warmth emanating from her husband's body. He held her tightly against him, and there was no way to ignore the growing arousal that pressed into her belly. It seemed to take forever for her shivers to calm, but finally she felt her skin tingling, the signal that her circulation was returning.

Lifting her head from Rogan's chest, she looked at him. He stared right back at her with such intensity that it made her belly leap inside of her. Her nipples hardened, and Marlie realized she wanted to rub herself against him.

She reached up and stroked his cheek. He closed his eyes and seemed to savor her touch. Marlie also lifted her leg against his underneath their blanket, prompting him to bend his knee and bring his leg up between hers to rest against her moist skin. She gasped and bit her lip at the contact.

Closing her own eyes, Marlie rocked her hips back and forth ever-so-gently against his leg, driving herself wild with the sudden need to make love to him, right there and then. Rogan inhaled deeply, and she knew he could smell exactly how aroused she was, but she didn't want to ruin this moment with words. The silence between them was almost magical.

Lowering her head, Marlie kissed the skin of his chest, darting her tongue out to taste him. He groaned, and his manhood pushed against her flesh. She responded by thrusting her hips, gasping when he joined her erotic game. Pressing his knee even harder against her, he tangled his hand in her hair and pulled back her head.

Rogan's eyes were on fire, flashing at her in the darkness. She knew what he wanted to know—if she was sure and if this was indeed what she wanted. Marlie answered his silent question by pulling his head down to hers, then kissing his lips and plunging her tongue into his mouth.

Before she knew what he'd done, she found herself pressed back into the carpet with Rogan lying on top of her. Feeling his delicious weight bearing down on her again was Heaven. The knee he'd kept between her legs now spread them apart as he settled there, nestled against her and fitting her body perfectly.

His mouth never left hers, but his hands wandered down her body, caressing her skin and making her buck against him. She'd been without him for so long that she was fierce in her need, clutching onto the back of his head and kissing him so deeply that her head spun.

When Rogan's hand found her breast, she moaned into his mouth, lifting herself up to him and silently begging for more of his touch. Her nipple was a stiff peak as he rubbed it between his fingers. But no matter how much she arched against him, he never touched the one place that throbbed for him. She desperately wanted him to and almost asked, but she still didn't want to break the silence between them for fear that he would stop.

And she didn't want him to stop.

Suddenly, Rogan's mouth was gone, and Marlie

only had a moment to ponder his intent before his hot mouth claimed the breast he'd just been fondling. Her skin was still cold to the touch, and the heat of his tongue was exquisite, burning her skin. Marlie gasped for breath, desperate to have him thrusting inside of her.

He would have moved on to her other breast, but she was too impatient to let him. Pulling him back to her mouth, she kissed him again, opening herself wide to him and caressing his thighs with hers. Just in case he didn't get the message, she let her hands wander down to his backside, squeezing him closer to her.

She could feel him grinding into her sensitive flesh. It wouldn't take much effort at all for him to pull back and plunge inside of her. He released her mouth and removed her hands from his hips only to thread his fingers through hers and press their hands into the carpet. Once again his eyes flashed, and Marlie sucked in her breath.

He pulled back only to poise himself at her entry. Bringing his lips close to her mouth, they barely fluttered on hers as he held her eyes and whispered, "You are *my* mate, Marlie Silver."

With that, he drove home, thrusting into her as deep as he could go. Marlie cried out at the feeling of him inside of her, clutching onto his hands with a vengeance. He continued to gaze at her with his flashing eyes as he pulled back and pushed forward again. When he did it a third time, Marlie's entire body shuddered as she planted her feet on the floor, lifting her hips up to him.

Again and again, Rogan slowly plunged inside her, grasping her hands tightly and never once looking away. At that moment, she realized what he was doing. He was marking her as his, claiming his territory right then and there, and telling her without a doubt that she belonged to him.

Marlie wanted to beg him to go faster, wanted to

plead for him to kiss her, but she knew he wouldn't. Rogan was doing more than merely making love to her—he was taking her and making damn sure she knew it. With each entry, his hardened flesh touched her deep inside, bringing her closer and closer to her climax. But he was taking his time, going slow and easy, and Marlie had to bite her lips to keep from demanding a faster pace.

But he knew exactly what she wanted. She was sure of it.

Rogan growled deep in his throat as he watched her breasts bouncing with each thrust and the passion that crossed her features when he was fully sheathed. Finally, he gave her exactly what she wanted—somehow knowing she was close to release. In and out, Rogan plunged faster and faster until Marlie couldn't take it anymore. Gripping his hands tightly, she cried out, falling over the edge and feeling the waves of pleasure radiate throughout her body. She couldn't help but lift her hips up to him, wanting to feel more and not being denied, because Rogan didn't stop his rhythm. Once Marlie opened her eyes, she could see him still watching her, groaning himself at her hooded eyes. At that moment, she knew he'd been waiting for her to come first.

With a growl and a deep thrust, he began a new rhythm, one that was purely predatory, that told her of the creature he could become. Releasing her hands, he kissed her savagely, grasping her hips and holding her up to receive him. His thrusts were fast and sharp, inciting another response from her. His hardened body slid into hers, pumping to the rhythm of Marlie's pounding heart. Once again, she drifted upward in her passion. Right after Rogan shuddered, calling out her name, she came once more, riding the waves of pleasure with him as he pressed hard and deep inside of her.

He continued to hold her hips to his, rolling back and forth in small thrusts, heightening her pleasure. Marlie couldn't think. She could barely even move other than to run her fingers through his hair. His forehead pressed against hers as he gazed into her eyes, and she could see for herself how pleased he was that he'd exerted his dominance.

She *was* his mate. No doubt about it.

Fifteen

"Take the ring off your neck," Rogan demanded in the darkness. He was still deep inside of her, pressing forward gently and making her gasp.

"Rogan…" Marlie whispered, unsure if she was speaking to him or to herself.

"Take it off," he said again, licking and sucking on her neck.

"Why?" she managed to ask, her voice sounding gritty to her own ears.

"Because you are mine, Marlie. My mate, my wife. You're covered with my scent, and I want you to wear my ring. On your finger."

Marlie gasped as she stared at him, running her hands through his hair. "You want me to put it back on?"

"Yes," he said, pushing forward again.

Marlie loved feeling him in her body, knowing they were one again.

"You will no longer hide your love for me," he said.

Blushing to her roots, Marlie glanced away from his

eyes.

"Don't be embarrassed, honey," he said, gently clutching her chin to bring her eyes back to his. "I know you still love me."

Marlie's eyes filled with tears, but she did not deny his words. "Will you put it back on my finger?" she asked in a small voice.

He gave her a wide grin. "Of course I will."

He pulled away from her, grabbing her hands and helping her into a sitting position. He made sure the blanket was still draped around them while Marlie reached behind her neck to unclasp the chain. Once she held it in her hand, Rogan took it from her and slipped the diamond ring from the necklace.

He took her left hand and pushed the ring onto her third finger. Marlie couldn't help but cry at the gesture. It had been so long since she'd worn it that it felt foreign to her, but so very wonderful at the same time.

"Now I'll never take it off," she whispered to him, gazing at the ring.

Rogan framed her face with his hands. He looked deeply into her eyes and said, "No matter where this life takes me, Marlie, will you follow me? Will you be there for me?"

Marlie reached up and grasped his hands on her face, making sure he couldn't pull away. "Wherever you go, I'll be right there with you. I don't care if you're Matthew Silver or Rogan Wolfe. No matter what name you have, I'm still your wife."

"Can you live like this?" he asked. "Can you live not knowing where you're going to sleep at night? Not knowing if tomorrow is the day you might die?"

"I don't know," she answered truthfully. "All I know, Rogan, is that I don't ever want to be separated from you again. When you died, I died too. Now that you're alive,

I'm alive again. And now that we've... that we've made love," she said with a blush, "I'm reminded of how much I love you."

Rogan took a deep breath and held it, closing his eyes before expelling it. When he opened them once more, he smiled and said, "Then we've got a lot of lost time to catch up on."

Marlie grinned. "That we do, Mr. Wolfe. That we do."

She leaned into his lips and kissed him.

~ * ~

"How's your leg?"

Marlie's soft voice penetrated Rogan's thoughts as she lay on top of him later. Her sweet scent surrounded him, and he breathed in deeply.

"Feels better," he said, tucking a stray hair behind her ear.

"I should take a look at it. You've given those stitches quite the beating in the past few hours."

"I'll be fine," he told her, not wanting to move. He was perfectly comfortable right where he was. Making love to Marlie had rocked him, and all he wanted to do was hold her in his arms, keep her safe and warm.

He couldn't believe his possessive feelings toward her, so strong even after being reunited with Marlie for only a short time. He wanted to make sure she was well aware that he was back in her life to stay. Thinking back on his memories from his life before, he knew more than ever that he'd made love to her long ago. Passionately, lovingly. Marlie was a beautiful, desirable woman, and it floored him that she hadn't been with another man since his supposed death. He smiled, knowing she truly belonged to him.

"I need to look at it anyway, Rogan," Marlie said, snapping his thoughts back to the subject at hand. "You could have busted some of them."

With a sigh, he relented, sitting up against the couch. Not too far away, a lamp sat on the floor. Marlie turned the switch and, amazingly, it blinked on.

"Guess they haven't turned the power off yet," she said, avoiding his eyes. He could smell her bashfulness as she blushed under his scrutiny.

Rogan relaxed and stared at her naked before him. He'd never get tired of looking at her. She was beautiful with her creamy skin and breasts that beckoned his tongue. His eyes wandered down her frame, coming to rest at the patch of curls at the top of her thighs.

"What?" Marlie asked, noticing where his gaze was set.

"I just thought of something."

"What?" she asked again.

"I remember the taste of your mouth, sweetheart," he whispered, lifting the corner of his lips. "But I don't remember how the rest of you tastes."

Marlie cleared her throat. It was obvious to him that he'd caught her off guard. He enjoyed talking sexy to her. She never failed to reward him with her lovely surprised scent.

"Well, I… you…"

She was so clearly flustered that Rogan couldn't help but chuckle at her.

"I bet you taste as sweet as candy," he said, running the pad of his finger down her cheek. "Warm honey just waiting for me to feast on."

His finger made a trail between her breasts as he spoke. Marlie shuddered, and he could clearly smell her desire once again. But before she let his hand wander down to her slick skin, she grabbed it, stopping its descent.

"I *need* to check your stitches," she said in a voice that didn't sound too convincing. "You're distracting me."

"Is it working?" he asked, winking at her.

"God, yes!"

Rogan chuckled. "Then hurry up, woman. I'm hungry, and I've got a sweet tooth."

Marlie gasped and blushed a deep crimson, but she couldn't hide the smile when she bit her lips. Drawing back the blanket, she gasped again, seeing for herself what Rogan's own thoughts had done to him. Even though they'd made love not too long before, he was already hard and ready to go again.

She was trying to divert her eyes from his length, but time and again her gaze rested on him, making him groan.

"How do the stitches look, Doc?" he asked in a tense voice. He laced his fingers together and put his hands behind his head to keep them from reaching out and touching her.

"I don't believe it!" she exclaimed.

"What?" he asked, glancing at his leg.

"You're almost completely healed. I mean, your wounds will be sore for a bit, but new scar tissue has already grown over them. I need to remove your stitches."

"I told you we healed fast."

"I didn't know you meant *this* fast," she retorted.

"By the time we meet up with Sean again, he'll be just as healed as I am. Except, unlike me, he'll be setting off metal detectors all over town."

Rogan regretted his attempt at humor almost immediately. In an instant, Marlie's languid demeanor changed, and he sensed her entire body tense.

"Do you think he'll find us?" she asked in a small voice, her eyes wide. "Jesus, Rogan. What do you think he did to Wade?"

Rogan cursed himself when he saw tears in her eyes. "I don't know, honey," he said gently. "But he didn't kill him, that's for sure. If he wanted him dead, he would have shot him with a bullet, not a dart."

"But why? Didn't you say you liberated the

B*E*A*S*T* compound?"

"We did, but that doesn't mean the benefactors of B*E*A*S*T* don't want us dead. Or worse, returned to be reprogrammed."

"Do you think that's what will happen to Wade?"

"I hope not, Marlie," he said with a sigh. "If that's what Wade's got to look forward to, then it would have been better if he'd been shot with a bullet."

Marlie shivered and turned away. Pulling the blanket off her shoulders, she stood and wandered into the kitchen.

"Where are you going?" he asked, craning his neck to catch a glimpse of her backside.

"To see if these people left any scissors behind," she said over her shoulder. "I need to cut those stitches."

Rogan rubbed his eyes. He should have kept his mouth shut. Now the mood between them was ruined. Damn it.

Sixteen

Sean sniffed the air. Even in his shifted state, he couldn't figure out where the hell Rogan and the woman had gone. Inhaling deeply, he leapt into the waters of the fast-moving creek and waded downstream. After long minutes with no sign of Rogan's scent, he turned around.

He didn't come this way, Sean thought with a growl. The wolf's stink was nowhere to be found. He doubted Rogan had stayed in the creek for too long—not when he was towing his wife behind him.

The icy water raced past Sean's paws, hardly fazing him. Looking down at himself, his abilities never ceased to amaze him. Bears had been hunting salmon in frigid waters since the dawn of time, and he was no exception. Sean loved being a shifter, and he was glad they'd made him a grizzly. He loved the power, the strength, and the heightened senses it gave him, even when he was human. And he especially loved being able to think as a human while in his shifted state.

His gunshot wounds gave him a few twinges here and there, but they were healing fast. Rogan was still going to pay. Now Sean had to live with who knows how many shotgun pellets in his hide, not to mention the scar he already bore on his face—all thanks to that damned traitor.

A scent drifted to him on the wind. *A wolf!* Sean's heart sprang to life as he bounded through the water, but suddenly he stopped cold, continuing to chuff at the air. That wasn't Rogan's scent. *Shit!*

A pack of wolves must be nearby. With another growl, Sean climbed the bank on the far side of the creek and tried to pick up Rogan's trail once more. The bastard was sneaky, he'd give him that. But Sean wasn't about to lose him.

No chance in hell.

~ * ~

Wade opened his eyes and groaned, seeing nothing but darkness surrounding him. His wrists were tied behind his back, and when he pulled on them, he could feel that they were somehow attached to his ankles. *Shit.* The sonofabitch had hogtied him!

His mind was cloudy, but he still couldn't shift no matter how hard he tried. Wade knew from experience that the serum only lasted four hours at most. That meant he hadn't been out for too long.

Closing his eyes, Wade tried to clear his mind. Once he opened them again, he squinted into the darkness, finally able to see shapes. He was in the back of a Hummer that stunk to high Heaven of Sean.

Wade was really beginning to hate these damned trucks. Just like the one he'd shared with Rogan, this one didn't have a back seat. He couldn't see much more with his human eyes. If he'd been able to shift, he could have seen a lot more with his keen cougar's vision. But it was a dark night, and he could barely see the back of the driver's seat.

Fortunately, Sean was nowhere to be seen. And the fact that neither Rogan nor Marlie were hogtied in the truck with him meant that Sean hadn't succeeded in finding them yet. Unless he'd already killed them.

But Wade doubted that. If Sean had been successful in his mission, there was no doubt in his mind that the damned grizzly would be behind the wheel, crowing like a rooster over his victory and driving Wade back to the Hell he'd come from.

"Christ!" he exclaimed through gritted teeth.

Twisting this way and that, Wade grunted when the ropes cut into his skin. His hands were probably blue from lack of circulation. In this position, it was hard for him to use any of his strength as a shifter to break free, probably exactly why Sean had tied him that way. But Wade was determined not to make things too easy for him.

Glancing around on the floor of the truck, he smiled when he found what he sought—a bolt sticking up through the carpet where the non-existent backseat of the Hummer would have been attached to the frame. Rolling himself into position, Wade grunted as he began rubbing his bonds against it at a frantic pace. It would take forever to break free, but he had no other choice.

Wade whispered a prayer to all that was holy that he'd be able to escape and get away. He shuddered to think of what lay in store for him if he failed.

~ * ~

Sometime later, the rope holding Wade's hands finally snapped. A surge of joy ripped through his heart, and he brought his hands around in front of him. He grunted as his muscles screamed from being in one position for too long, but he didn't think too long on it before he began untying his ankles.

Crawling on all fours, Wade grimaced as he made his way to the front of the Hummer. He needed to get out of there, and fast. He may have been tranquilized, but he'd understood Sean when he'd been on his phone in the forest, and he'd heard Sean mention Brett. Biting his lip, Wade tried to remember exactly what had been said.

But just the thought of Brett made him shudder. He was a cheetah, clocked by B*E*A*S*T* at 75 miles per hour at a dead run. Not only that, Brett craved the taste of blood and made sure everyone knew it. He was almost as ruthless as Tam himself.

Sean had been upset, that much Wade could remember. Hadn't he said something about an old man? And Brett finding him out here in the wilderness? Wade wasn't an idiot; he knew why Sean hadn't killed him. The men behind B*E*A*S*T* didn't want him dead. But why?

Wade reached up to the driver's visor near the windshield and pulled it down. *Damn, nothing.* He'd hoped Sean would have left the keys in the truck. Heaving a deep sigh, he ran his fingers through his hair and climbed into the driver's seat. When he heard a soft jingling, his heart leapt into his throat.

With a shaking hand, he reached down to the ignition—and found the keys! Apparently, Sean hadn't stopped long enough to pull them out. A wide smile split Wade's face.

"Excellent," he whispered.

He opened the driver's side door and fell out into the snow. If he was going to get out of there, the first thing he needed to do was ditch the GPS locator beacon on Sean's truck. He lay on the snow, scooting underneath the Hummer near the left rear wheel. Hidden in the wheel-well was the device he sought, flashing every few seconds with a red light.

With a strong heave, it loosened. Again and again, Wade tried to dislodge it until it finally fell into his hand. He couldn't help the low chuckle that escaped him. With tremendous satisfaction, he pulled back his arm and threw the beacon for all he was worth into the tree line.

"Catch me now, you wily bastard," he growled

under his breath right before he jumped into the truck. The engine roared to life and, without looking back, Wade pulled out onto the highway and sped toward Anchorage.

Seventeen

Marlie returned a few minutes later, a look of consternation on her face.

"What's the matter?"

With a sigh, she plopped down onto the couch next to Rogan. "This was all I could find." She held up a pair of toenail clippers.

"Better than nothing, right?" he asked with a wink.

"I guess so. Give me that leg."

Rogan swung it up onto her lap and grinned. Marlie tried desperately to concentrate on the task at hand. But her eyes were pulled like magnets to the scar on the inside of his thigh.

"Do you remember how you got that?" she asked as she began the tedious task of cutting the sutures.

"I told you, honey," Rogan said, his eyes flashing in the warm glow of the lamp, "all I can remember from my life before is making love to you."

Marlie swallowed hard then took a deep breath. "You were climbing a fence," she said in a soft voice. "There was barbed wire on the top of it, but you were trying to impress a girl. So you climbed over it anyway."

Rogan threw back his head and laughed at that. "By the looks of this scar, I don't think I impressed her much."

With a smile, Marlie said, "Oh, I don't know. She was scared shitless. Ran all the way home to tell her parents. Left you out in the middle of nowhere bleeding all over creation."

"Well, did her parents come to my rescue?"

She nodded. "Yup. Took you to the hospital even."

"Is that so?" he asked with an arched brow. "How is it that you know so much about it?"

"It was me."

"It was *you*?" He sounded shocked.

"Yes, I was the girl you were trying to impress. We've known each other for a long time."

Rogan stared at her as if trying to process her words. "How long?"

Marlie pulled out the last of his stitches as she said, "I met you in middle school. I was fourteen and you were fifteen, a grade above me. But I worshipped you."

Rogan gave her a knowing grin. "You did?"

"Oh, yeah," she said, staring off into space. "You're the only man I've ever loved. My one and only." Silence greeted her words, and she brought her gaze back to him, shuddering at the look in his eyes.

"You've never been with anyone else?" he whispered.

Marlie shook her head. "I lost my virginity to you, along with my heart… and my soul."

Rogan pulled his leg off of her lap and advanced on her, pushing her down into the couch cushions. Simply gazing into his beautiful eyes made crazy things happen in her belly. Instantly she was wet for him even though he hadn't touched her, and she opened her legs to allow him access.

"Everything I am belongs to you," she whispered up

to him, stroking his cheek.

Rogan groaned, laying his forehead on her shoulder. "Marlie…"

"What?" She felt his fingers press into her wet folds, slipping inside of her.

"I want to taste you here," he said.

His words alone made her muscles clench inside of her. She gasped, fisting her hand in his hair.

"Will you let me?"

Marlie sucked in her breath when she witnessed Rogan pull his fingers away from her, only to swirl them around one of her nipples, slicking it with her own wetness. And when he laved that same breast, suckling it deep into his mouth, flicking the tip of her with his tongue, it nearly drove her mad. She craved his body within hers once more but nearly came apart at his next words.

"Dear God, woman. You taste so sweet." His flashing eyes held hers while his tongue flicked her nipple, and she couldn't help but arch into him. "You like my tongue on you?"

Marlie nodded furiously. Rogan chuckled.

"Do you want my tongue here?" he asked, once again delving into her with his fingers.

She nodded once more.

"Say it, babe. Ask me."

Holy… Rogan wanted her to beg him? Marlie couldn't swallow her thundering heart no matter how hard she tried.

"Please…" she whispered.

"Please what?" he answered, flicking her again and biting the peak of her breast gently.

"Rogan," she whined. "Please."

"Please what, darlin'? I'll give you what you want. You just gotta ask."

Panting, Marlie bit her lip. Her entire body cried out

for his touch. She wasn't above begging—was she?

"Please put your mouth on me. Taste me, Rogan. Oh, God… I want your mouth between my legs."

That was all he needed to begin his descent. Lower and lower he went, licking and biting her quivering belly while caressing her thighs. Marlie groaned as she watched him, her entire body shivering with eager anticipation.

"Sit up," he commanded, pulling her hips to the side of the couch.

"What?" she asked, her brain in a fog.

"Sit up, honey," he said again, running his hands up her inner thighs and pulling her legs apart.

Marlie did as he said, throwing back her head onto the cushions.

"Can you smell that?" he whispered.

"Smell what?"

"Your sweet musk. It's making my mouth water."

That comment brought her eyes back to his. They flashed a bright gold color, only for a second, but it was there. Her heart slammed against her ribcage, and she was reminded again that Rogan was a shifter—a wolf. Marlie sucked in her breath.

"Don't be afraid," he said, holding her gaze while his fingers gently played against her.

"But you're a—"

"I know what I am," he said. "I am your *mate*—the man you've given your soul to. You just said as much. Do you deny it now?"

His fingers slowly pushed inside of her, and she involuntarily scooted closer to press against him.

"No!" she gasped.

"Then let me make love to you, Marlie. Watch as I fill you with my tongue."

Dipping his head, Rogan crouched between her legs, slowly delving his tongue into her wetness, replacing his fingers with his mouth. Marlie moaned in ecstasy at the contact, once again throwing back her head.

"Don't look away." Rogan's deep voice vibrated through her. "Watch me, sweetheart."

Marlie blushed but complied, looking down as he began again, swirling around her swollen flesh, lapping hungrily. Gazing at him while he pleasured her was so erotic that every nerve ending in her body prickled with excitement. Up and down, his head bobbed, and her hips followed him in his rhythm. Rogan pushed her legs farther apart as he pressed closer, attacking her mercilessly. Just as she was about to climax, he pulled away and looked up at her, grinning devilishly.

"I remember," he said, his mouth glistening. "I *remember*, Marlie. Dear God in Heaven."

"Rogan…" she panted, sure she was going to come at his words alone. But he didn't return his mouth to her. Instead, he began sensually kissing her inner thighs. "What are you doing?" she demanded.

"Bringing out the wild woman in you," he said right before he leapt up and pounced on her with lightning speed, kissing her into oblivion.

Marlie didn't even have time to squeal before his mouth was on hers, his tongue demanding entry. She could taste herself on his lips and whimpered, trying in vain to press herself against him.

"Roll over," he whispered into her ear once he released her mouth.

Marlie was beyond caring what he was going to do. She was teetering on the edge of sanity. She turned over, her body throbbing with the need to release as Rogan helped her to lie over the arm of the couch, then he pulled her backside against him, entering her from behind.

"Oh, God!" Marlie inadvertently clenched her muscles.

Rogan groaned loudly and thrust again, reaching his hand around her hips to massage her slick skin with his fingers. Again and again Marlie pressed backwards into him, wanting desperately to feel the fullness of him inside of her.

Rogan's other arm curled around her only to tease and pull on one of her nipples. But it wasn't until he bit her neck that she finally came, exploding around him, straining for more. Clutching onto his arm, she held on tight as her shudders continued, prolonged by the sound of him growling his release in her ear.

When the glory of their lovemaking receded, Marlie could have sworn she saw stars swirling about her head. She chuckled at the thought.

"What's so funny?" Rogan asked as he sat back, pulling her along with him onto his lap, still firmly rooted within her depths.

"I'm lightheaded," she whispered, leaning her head back onto his shoulder. "I don't ever remember making love to you quite like that before."

"Is that good or bad?"

"Oh, honey," she said, lacing her fingers with his. "It's definitely *all* good."

Rogan moved her hair and kissed her neck up and down, making her shiver. "That's what I like to hear," he said, his grin of satisfaction clearly evident in his voice.

Turning her head, Marlie gave him a kiss she hoped he could read—a kiss full of love.

Suddenly, Rogan pulled away roughly and inhaled.

"What's the matter?" she asked, caressing his face.

"Shit! Marlie, get up—now!"

"But, Rogan…"

"Now!" Rogan pushed her off his lap. "Grab our clothes and get the hell upstairs!"

"What's going on?" she yelled.

Before he could answer, a thunderous crash

suddenly shook the house. A deep, growling roar could be heard from the dining room, making every hair on Marlie's body stand on end.

"It's Sean!" Rogan screamed.

Eighteen

Rogan watched as Marlie scrambled up the stairs with her arms full of their clothes. She fell a few times, crying her eyes out and screaming in terror. Rogan didn't blame her. A bolt of fear had raced up *his* spine the moment he'd seen that giant bear growling at him from the edge of the living room.

Sean wasn't advancing—not yet anyway. He stood there snarling, probably trying his best to intimidate Rogan with his long, sharp teeth. Rogan just hoped he'd be able to preoccupy Sean long enough for Marlie to get herself dressed.

"You want to kill me. Don't you, Sean?" Rogan taunted him, knowing full well the bear could understand his words. A loud growl filled the room in reply. "Then I *dare* you to do it!"

Sean stood on his hind legs with a roar, but was hindered by the ceiling. He dropped to all fours and began to charge. Rogan leapt away, shifting at the same time.

The sound of his bones popping in his ears was deafening as they morphed and changed shape. His skin itched when the heavy grey fur grew, and suddenly he was more agile, leaping over the side table just as the bear swiped at him. Rogan's new wolf body raced through the lower floor of the house, keeping the bear occupied. He knew he didn't have much time to get to Marlie. The house had too many places where the great bear could corner him.

But as Rogan bounded over the counter in the kitchen, he realized sending Marlie upstairs hadn't been his brightest idea. Just how the hell were they supposed to escape? Growling to himself, he skidded on the Pergo floor, leaving long claw marks behind him. He could almost feel Sean breathing down his neck as he sprang up the stairs, sending up a prayer of thanks that the staircase wasn't wide enough for a Kodiak grizzly.

But it wouldn't take Sean long to figure out that all he had to do was shift in order to race up the stairs after him.

~ * ~

Sean roared with rage. White foam dangled from his mouth as he tried to shoulder his way up the stairs to no avail. He'd have to shift. *Goddamn it!*

Shaking the house once again with his mighty roar, Sean's body began changing shape. He couldn't shift fast enough. Without waiting for his body to fully transform back into his human state, Sean raced up the stairs, his arms and legs still covered with grizzly hair, his face halfway elongated into a bear's snout.

"Rogan!" he yelled, the sound of his voice not quite human.

The moment he'd picked up Rogan's scent in the woods, his vision had turned red. Nothing else in the world mattered at that point. He'd been choked with fury, pounding through the snow with a vengeance. Once he saw the dark house in front of him, he'd known it was where they were holed up. And the stench of their disgusting sexcapades had almost made him vomit.

Regardless, Sean grinned evilly. He knew he would

be victorious. There would be no escape this time.

~ * ~

Marlie had quickly donned her sweater and still-wet pants without bothering with her bra or undies. She even managed to slip on her soggy shoes. While she'd frantically dressed at the top of the stairs, one of the syringes of serum had dropped out of Rogan's pocket and fallen onto the floor. She stared at it for a moment before snatching it up in her shaking hand along with the rest of their clothing.

With frightened tears in her eyes, she remembered what Rogan had told her. This serum prevented the shifters from changing their shape. Maybe it could work to their advantage!

Rogan thundered up the stairs with Sean hot on his tail. Marlie watched in horror as Sean began to shift, not bothering to return completely to his human form. She could hardly hold back a scream as he slowly climbed the stairs growling Rogan's name.

The huge wolf beside her put his body between her and the advancing bear. Rogan snarled, pushing her back against the far wall.

"Rogan, I have the serum!" she yelled, wondering whether or not her husband could truly understand her.

Instantly the wolf began to shift, and within moments, the form of Rogan stood in front of her once again. He took the syringe from her hand.

"Get out of here, Marlie."

"But—"

"Do *NOT* argue with me. I'll find you. Take my clothes and jump out the window. *I'll find you!*" As he spoke, he pushed her through the door of the master bedroom right before he launched himself at Sean.

Marlie clutched the clothing to her chest and raced for the bedroom window. She could hear the two men as they crashed down the stairs, and more tears blurred her vision. Her heart raced and she found herself praying that Rogan would make it out alive. She could *not* lose him now!

As she tried to open the window, it finally cracked open. With a shove, she pushed it up, rejoicing when she saw the roof of the garage right outside. Frantic sobs racked her as she punched out the screen and scrambled out onto the shingles. More than once, she almost lost her footing, and when the cold air hit her, she realized she'd left Wade's jacket in the living room. Damn it!

Instantly her shivers returned, and her wet pants became uncomfortable. The soft, powdery snow on the rooftop clung to her legs, and she gasped as she wandered closer to the ledge. Dear God, she was supposed to *jump*? She didn't know if she could, and she began to hyperventilate.

"I can't do this. *I can't do this!*"

Swallowing hard, she scooted closer to the edge, her heart thundering in her chest. But before she could muster the courage to jump, her foot slipped out from under her and removed the need for courage. With a shriek, Marlie fell over the side into the snow on the front lawn.

A blinding pain shot through her ankle. She could barely catch her breath as she lay there sobbing and clutching at her leg, but the commotion inside the house made her scramble to her feet. As soon as she tried to put weight on her right ankle, she fell over, screaming in the process. Setting her jaw, Marlie got up again and grabbed the clothing she'd dropped. If she could just make it to the tree line, she'd be okay. At least, that's what she hoped. With the throbbing in her leg, she doubted she'd be able to get much father than that.

It was dark outside. More clouds were in the sky, obstructing the moon's glow. She would have given anything to have some moonlight reflecting off the snow. Each step was excruciating as she tried to run. The trees were so close, but they seemed so damned far away!

Marlie stumbled over a rock hidden in the snow and fell, crying dejectedly. She had no idea what was going on with Rogan, if he was winning or losing. Her ankle ached like a son of a bitch, and she seriously doubted she could make it to the tree line on her own.

A chirping sound suddenly emerged from Rogan's pants, making her squeal and jump. When it chirped again, she realized it was a ring tone. Rogan's cell phone was ringing!

As she sat there in the snow, Marlie fumbled with his pants until she finally pulled the phone out and flipped it open.

"Hello?" she answered breathlessly.

~ * ~

Just as Rogan leapt at Sean, he bit the plastic covering off the syringe of serum and turned it in his hand. Launching himself off the first step, he crashed into Sean's body, making him fall backward down the stairs. Sean's half-shifted body was as solid as a rock as they crashed down hard, and Rogan couldn't help his howl of satisfaction when he felt the tip of the needle pierce Sean's neck and heard him scream with rage. Rogan pushed the serum directly into his bloodstream.

Once they'd tumbled to the bottom of the stairs, Sean landed on top of him, snarling and snapping at his face. Rogan rolled back and forth, just barely avoiding Sean's horrifying visage.

"What did you do to me, you bastard?" Sean yelled with a growl, his deep, unnatural voice raising the hair on the back of Rogan's neck.

"I made sure you couldn't shift!"

Out of nowhere, one of Sean's meaty fists slammed into Rogan's cheek so hard he saw stars explode behind his eyes. With a mighty heave, Rogan pushed him off, shoving him back just enough to crawl out from under him. Sean tried to slam into Rogan once more, but Rogan was quicker and leapt over the couch. As he hit the floor, he rolled toward the wall and came face to face with Marlie's shotgun—still propped up right where he'd left it!

Rogan grabbed it and pointed it at Sean before the bastard could even round the couch. The sound of the cocking hammer filled the room. Sean was visibly seething, and Rogan could see the foam dripping from his mouth as he stood there in apparent indecision.

"You better kill me first, Wolfe," Sean said as he advanced. "Otherwise I'm going to rip you to pieces, then what will that pretty wife of yours do when I come for her?"

"Leave her out of this."

"Not a chance."

"This is between you and me. Marlie has nothing to do with any of it!"

"Oh, she has *everything* to do with it," Sean said with a sneer, slowly advancing. "You don't seem to understand. I get to you through her."

"You son of a—"

Rogan lifted the gun and aimed, but he hesitated as he remembered the sound of the screaming guards he'd shackled to the wall at the B*E*A*S*T* compound not too long ago. He hadn't killed them, but he might as well have. He'd released all the shifters from their cells, and *they* were the ones who'd ripped those men apart. Now the memory of it forced bile to rise in the back of his throat.

He wasn't a killer. Even though he knew Sean wouldn't hesitate to shoot him if the tables were turned, Rogan couldn't bring himself to kill the man before him. Sean continued to advance, the smile on his twisted face looking more like a grimace.

"Look at you. You're a pussy," Sean said. "Do it, Wolfe. Or don't you have the balls to kill me?"

"I'm not like you. I don't kill people."

"That's too damn bad. You know, I remember your friend Justin. Tasted like chicken. Mmm, that pretty bird tasted so good. I must admit though, I've never had a wolf. And my belly is growling."

Sean flew through the air, clearly intent on bringing Rogan down. Making a split-second decision, Rogan swung the shotgun at him like a baseball bat, hitting him square in the temple. Sean went down hard, smacking into the floor with a resounding thud.

He didn't appear to be moving, but Rogan wasn't taking any chances. Turning the gun in his hands, he struck the butt of the weapon against Sean's head again with a sickening crack. If he wasn't out before, he certainly was now.

"That's for Justin, you son of a bitch," Rogan said through a snarl, wiping a few drops of blood from his nose.

He raced through the house and found a few towels in the linen closet that he ripped to shreds and used to bind Sean's wrists behind his back. Then he bound his ankles. Rogan had no idea how long that would hold him, but he hoped to God it would be long enough.

Nineteen

"Marlie? Is that you?"

"Wade!" Marlie's eyes were open wide as she gasped into the phone, recognizing the voice on the other end. "Where are you? Are you all right?"

"Yeah, yeah. Don't worry about me. Sean tied me up and left me, but I was able to break free and steal his truck. Where are you guys?"

"I… I don't know!" Marlie wailed, glancing behind her at the house a few yards away. "We're in some housing tract. Rogan's fighting with Sean!"

"Shit! You don't have a clue where you are? I can come get you!"

Looking around frantically, Marlie wiped the tears from her eyes and squinted as she saw a sign not too far away from her.

"The Willow Brook housing development," she said. "That's what the sign says."

"Willow Brook? I passed that turnoff just a few minutes ago. Let me flip this bitch and I'll be right there. Hang on, Marlie. Okay? I'll be right there."

"Hurry, Wade. I don't know if he's… he's…" She

couldn't get any further as more sobs choked her.

"I will, sweetie. Just hang on."

Marlie snapped the phone shut, trembling more with fear than at the chilly air. "Please. Please hurry, Wade," she whispered.

~ * ~

It didn't take long for Wade to find the turnoff to Willow Brook. He raced down the winding road probably faster than was safe, but he didn't care. If Sean was beating on Rogan, Wade had no time to lose.

Marlie had sounded terrified on the phone, and Wade pressed a little harder on the accelerator. He wouldn't be able to live with himself if Sean somehow managed to hurt Rogan or his wife.

After a few minutes of driving, he finally saw houses in the distance. There, on the snow a few dozen yards from one of the houses, sat Marlie, waving her arms at him. Wade didn't waste any time barreling up the snowy grass, circling her so that the Hummer sat between her and the dark house behind her. If Sean came running out of the house, he didn't want him to have a clear line to Marlie.

Wade ripped open the driver side door and dropped to the snow. "What's wrong? Are you hurt?"

Marlie was crying too hard to speak. She merely nodded and pointed to her ankle. He could smell her pain, so he scooped her up into his arms and walked to the back of the truck to open the rear doors.

She clung to him, hugging him with a vengeance as she cried over and over, "Wade, Wade! You've got to help Rogan. You've got to—"

"Right now, I'm going to get *you* looked after," he said, making sure she was sitting back on the floor. "Are you comfortable?" She nodded, and he grabbed Sean's tranquilizer gun lying next to her. Making sure it was loaded, he handed it to her and said, "You shoot anything that comes through that door that isn't a wolf or a cougar. You got that?"

Marlie nodded again as she snatched the gun, holding it to her chest like a frightened child. But just as Wade turned to charge into the house and save the day, Rogan bounded out of the front door, his wolf paws decimating the snow as he ran with a shotgun in his mouth. Wade couldn't help the wide smile that lit up his face.

"Rogan!" he exclaimed.

"Rogan!" Marlie sounded desperate, and she would have scooted out of the Hummer if Wade hadn't stopped her.

Rogan bounded toward them, dropping the gun in the snow at Wade's feet just before he leapt into the back of the truck. Wade could see Marlie hugging him before he even had a chance to shift, throwing her arms around his furry neck. Wade grabbed the gun and threw it in after him, slamming the rear doors and rounding the truck to the driver's side. Once he'd climbed in, he glanced into the rearview mirror. Rogan had shifted back into his human form and was hugging his wife while he cried with her.

Wade didn't say a word, he merely put the Hummer in drive and raced back up Willow Brook Drive, snow flying into the air behind them.

~ * ~

Marlie's entire body trembled as she held on to Rogan, refusing to let him go even for a second. He'd shifted in her arms, a sensation that had been so foreign to her, but she didn't question it. She was just relieved to be holding him again. She heard him murmuring in her ear, telling her they were safe and were all right now. She calmed down somewhat, taking in deep gulps of air.

"Are… are you huh-hurt?" she asked, her teeth chattering.

"No, baby. I'm not." His soothing voice washed over her like a caress.

She looked up at him and gasped when she saw an angry purple bruise on his cheek. She covered it with her palm and said, "But you *are* hurt!"

Rogan took her hand away, bringing it to his mouth. "Not really. I'll be fully healed in a few hours, sweetheart. It's nothing to worry about. Sean punched me, that's all."

"Did you kill the bastard?" Wade's voice drifted over to them from behind the wheel.

Rogan hesitated a moment before he answered. "No. I didn't kill him. Knocked him out cold, but I didn't kill him."

"But he'll keep coming—"

"I'm not a killer, Wade!" Rogan's muscles tensed visibly, and Marlie's eyes widened at his sudden change in demeanor. "I refuse to become the animal B*E*A*S*T* engineered me to be. I tied him up and left him."

After Rogan's outburst, an oppressive silence overcame them all.

~ * ~

After a few minutes of basking in Marlie's embrace, Rogan moved her aside to root around for his clothing.

"How'd you find us?" he asked Wade, his tone calmer as he donned his jeans.

"I called your cell. Marlie answered."

"Good thing we bought these phones, eh?"

"No doubt," Wade agreed, nodding.

"How did you escape?"

Wade told them how he freed himself, and Rogan looked impressed. "Must have taken you forever."

Wade shrugged. "I don't remember how long it took. I just remember praying that Sean wouldn't come back."

Rogan took a deep breath and sighed, reaching into one of the bins lining the walls of the Hummer. He pulled out a B*E*A*S*T* issued black T-shirt, lifting it up and over his head. The agency was always sure to provide extra clothing in their trucks for the shifters in case they were needed after an "assignment."

"Sean wants me dead," Rogan said.

"That much is obvious." Wade chuckled, glancing at him in the rearview mirror.

"He wants Marlie dead too."

Marlie gasped and covered her mouth, and Rogan saw her begin to shiver again. Once he was fully dressed, he reached for her. She collapsed against him, as if being close to him could melt away all of her terror.

"Why is he… so hell-bent on killing *me* as well?" she asked in a small voice.

Rogan stroked her hair, and she closed her eyes. "I think in his mind you and I are one unit. He wants *you* to get to *me*. If he kills you, he'll be torturing me. But even if he gets to me first, I think he'd still come after you. The man's not stable, honey."

"Then what the hell are we going to do?"

Leaning back to look into her dark brown eyes, he saw them swimming with tears. Biting her lip, Marlie stroked his cheek.

"We're gonna have to go into hiding," he said.

"Where?" Wade asked.

"We'll call Noah and see where he's at. I know he met up with a few other shifters who were hiding in the mountains when we left Lanie's family cabin. I think there'll be safety in numbers. Sean's just one shifter. If we can band together, he won't stand a chance against us."

Wade cleared his throat. "He's not the *only* one."

"What do you mean?"

"After he shot me with the tranq, I heard Sean talking on his cell phone. He mentioned meeting up with Brett."

"Brett? Brett Walker?"

"I assume so."

Rogan ran his fingers through his hair and sighed. "Christ."

"Who's Brett Walker?" Marlie asked.

"He's another shifter—a cheetah. He was good friends with Tam, a ruthless son of a bitch if there ever was one."

"And Tam is the—"

"The black panther that went after Noah. Now, I guess Brett and Sean are in cahoots."

"I don't know about that," Wade said. "Sean didn't sound too happy about meeting up with him. But he mentioned an old man who wanted the cougar. Must have been talking about me."

"Either that or he's a fan of John Cougar Mellencamp." Marlie's soft voice filled the cabin, and both men glanced at her.

Rogan began to chuckle, and Wade cracked a grin at her lame joke.

"Even under the threat of imminent death, your wife still has a sense of humor, Wolfe."

Rogan gave her a squeeze and nuzzled her neck. Marlie's scent suddenly changed to one of yearning, and he groaned softly in response.

"That just means I got myself a good woman."

"That you do," Wade said, nodding in agreement.

Marlie blushed and hid her face in Rogan's neck.

Twenty

"Rogan? Is that you?"

"Noah, you old bastard! How you doing?" Rogan cracked a wide grin at finally connecting to Noah's phone. They'd reached Anchorage not too long before, stopping only long enough to eat some fast food in the cab of the Hummer. It was late, and the city of Anchorage had already rolled up the sidewalks.

"Hot damn, it is really you," Noah said. "Haven't heard from you in a few weeks, buddy, and I thought something might have happened to you. Did you ever find that wife of yours?"

"Yeah, I found her." Rogan glanced at Marlie and winked. She smiled and looked away, but her scent said it all. He'd embarrassed her again.

"Well?" Noah asked.

"Well what?"

"Well, do I have to kick it out of you? How did it go? How was your reunion?"

"I got shot."

"Jesus!"

"I'm okay now. It only hurt for a little while. But

Marlie seems to be taking things well. She's wearing her wedding ring again."

"That's wonderful! So she wasn't remarried I take it."

"Nope. Found out she was still pining away for me after all this time."

"Rogan!" Marlie squealed, hitting his shoulder.

"That her?" Noah asked, his tone telling Rogan he was smiling.

"The one and only."

"How's she taking the news that you're a shifter?"

"Quite well, actually. She was freaked out there for a little while. She's a vet, and so I shifted in order for her to dig the shotgun pellets out of my flank. I think I scared the bejesus out of her."

"But she's accepted you?"

"For the most part," Rogan said with a grin, stealing a quick kiss. "The good thing is that I remembered exactly how she tastes."

Marlie's eyes went wide as her scent suddenly turned from embarrassment to anger. She closed her fist and punched him this time.

"Ow!" Rogan exclaimed.

Noah chuckled into the phone. "Better watch that mouth of yours, Wolfe. Gets you into trouble every time."

"True enough. Listen, Noah. I called because I need to know where you are. Marlie and I are in a bit of trouble."

Silence answered him for a few moments before Noah said, "What's going on?"

"Sean's found us."

"Shit."

"Yeah. I guess he's been tracking Wade and me for some time now. He destroyed Marlie's house, and we have nowhere to go. We've got to get out of Alaska. I know you met up with a few of the escaped shifters before you left the

Rockies, and I thought maybe there'd be strength in numbers."

Noah cleared his throat. "I have no qualms about hooking up with you again, Wolfe, but there's something you should know."

"Oh? What's that?"

Noah's silence for a moment made him seem reluctant to answer.

"I didn't *only* meet up with a few shifters when Lanie and I left the mountains. We also came across a scientist from B*E*A*S*T*."

That shocked the shit out of Rogan. "Did you just say a—"

"A scientist, yeah. Took him awhile to convince us that he'd changed his tune, but he claims he hates B*E*A*S*T* almost as much as we do."

"Good Lord, Noah. You've got to be careful around this guy!"

"Don't worry. He's under twenty-four hour surveillance. Nobody trusts him. But he told us something that we all thought was worth checking out."

Rogan was almost too afraid to ask. "What?"

"The B*E*A*S*T* compound in Colorado—the one we destroyed—that's not the only one."

Rogan's blood ran cold. Holy shit, not the only one?

"What do you mean, Tiger?" Every nerve-ending in his body prickled, and his hands shook.

"I mean that, according to this scientist, there's a B*E*A*S*T* compound for every branch of the military."

"Oh my God."

"What is it, Rogan?" Marlie's voice broke into his racing thoughts, and he held a hand up to both her and Wade.

"Think about it, Rogan," Noah said. "You, me, Justin—we were all from the Marines. I'd be willing to bet

Wade was in the Marines as well."

"Dear God…"

"You ain't kiddin'."

"So, where are you guys?"

"We're in Portland, Oregon. This guy says the Air Force's compound is somewhere here in the Pacific Northwest. Lanie and I were traveling west anyhow, so we decided to check out his claim."

"Found any proof of it yet?"

"No, but the guys are looking. He's drawn us a map."

"How many shifters are with you?"

"Six others. They've been searching the Oregon countryside."

Rogan rubbed his eyes and sighed. "It's probably underground like the other one."

"Yeah. You guys are more than welcome to come help us check things out."

"You still have that scientist with you?"

"Oh, yeah. We aren't letting him out of our sight."

"Good. I'll call you when we get closer to Portland. We've got three drivers, so I don't think it'll take us that long. A few days at most. I thought about flying, but that would just generate too many questions about who we are. Besides, we snagged Sean's Hummer, so we're hooked up with tranquilizers, serum, guns, ammo, all kinds of goodies."

"Nice!" Noah said in appreciation. "I don't blame you for wanting to drive. Sounds like you scored."

"In more ways than one." Rogan once again winked at his wife.

"All right, Wolfe. I'm looking forward to seeing you again," Noah said. "Give your wife a kiss for me."

"Will do. And give Lanie two kisses—one from me and one from Wade."

Noah chuckled. "Sure thing. See you in a few days."

"Yup. Bye."

"Bye."

Taking a deep breath, Rogan snapped his phone shut and glanced back and forth between Marlie and Wade.

"We're in deep shit," he said.

"How deep?" Wade asked warily.

Rogan licked his lips. "According to Noah, the B*E*A*S*T* compound in Colorado wasn't the only one. They met up with a scientist in the Rockies who told them there was a compound for each branch of the military."

"Jesus *Christ!*"

"Yeah," Rogan agreed with a nod. "I think *He's* the only one who can help us now."

Twenty One

Sean awoke to a splitting headache. Twisting his body, he tried to recall where the hell he was and growled when he remembered Rogan. The bastard must have hit him over the head with the shotgun he'd been holding.

With another growl, Sean realized his hands and feet were bound. It didn't take much effort to rip his bonds and break free. Rogan's stench surrounded him, making him sick to his stomach. Looking down at his body, he could see he was still in his half-shifted state, and he couldn't change his form no matter how hard he tried. *Damn!* Rogan had injected him with the serum!

Sean couldn't hold back his rage. He destroyed everything in his path—the couch, the end table, even the kitchen counter. When it became apparent that Rogan and Marlie were no longer in the house, he ran outside through the front door, his hot breath puffing in the cold air.

Inhaling deeply, he could smell both of them along with another familiar scent. Once he realized what it was, Sean threw back his head and roared with fury.

Wade had escaped! *SHIT!*

Sean knew he'd be in for a severe tongue-lashing

from Covington. In the last few days, the old man had been more interested in capturing Wade than killing Rogan. Sean had no friggin' clue as to why, seeing as how Covington had wanted Wade dead a couple of weeks ago. And those traitorous bastards had stolen his truck! Just what the hell was he going to do *now*?

One thing was for sure: he wouldn't be able to go out in public until the serum wore off, and that wouldn't happen for at least another four hours, allowing enough time for Rogan's trail to turn cold. Bounding through the snow, Sean disappeared into the tree line, determined to find his clothing.

He was going to kill Rogan Wolfe, even if he killed *himself* doing it.

~ * ~

"Sir, you are *not* going to believe this."

Brett Walker sat in his black Jaguar on the shoulder of Glenn Highway with his cell phone to his ear. The Jag was a car that fit him, seeing as how he could shift into a cheetah. He prided himself on the fact that he had such tremendous speed. From a complete stand-still, Brett could easily beat any sports car on the market from zero to sixty in his shifted state. Granted, he couldn't sustain that speed for very long, but he'd been highly prized at B*E*A*S*T* because of it.

It was also one of the reasons Covington had sent him to Alaska. Sean had promised the old man he'd kill Rogan and capture Wade, and Brett was the lucky one Clive had chosen to bring the cougar back to Texas. If anything went wrong, he'd be able to catch Wade in his shifted state, no problem. Nothing on the planet could outrun a cheetah.

But, as Brett sat in his car with the engine running and the heater on full blast, he could only stare as he saw what he assumed to be Sean emerging from the woods. It looked like Sean, but he… wasn't quite himself.

"What?" came the voice on the other end of the cell. "What won't I believe?"

"I followed Sean's beacon up Glenn Highway, but his truck is gone. And… I've found Sean."

There was a short pause. "Is he dead?"

"Not… exactly."

"Then what the hell is going on?"

"I have no idea, sir. But it looks as if Sean is stuck between his human state and his bear state."

"What the hell?"

"Beats me, sir."

"Is there any sign of Wade or Rogan?"

"No, and their scent is faint. If they were here, it was a while ago. I can see the yellow Hummer they were using, but it's parked on the side of the road. I guess they abandoned it."

"Sean told me he'd drained their radiator. Probably overheated."

"It's possible."

"Look, go talk to Sean. I want to know what the hell is going on."

"You're the boss. I'll call you back."

Brett snapped the phone shut and turned off his car. He got out and crossed the road, pulling his trench coat tighter around his neck.

"Hey, Sean!"

Even Brett, despite all the horrors he'd seen at the B*E*A*S*T* compound, wasn't prepared for what Sean looked like up close. He stopped a few yards away.

"Jesus, Sean. What *happened* to you?"

Sean gulped a few huge breaths of air before answering him. "Rogan! That's what happened to me."

"Are you all right?"

"Do I look all right to you, Walker? Well, *DO I*?"

Brett held up his hands. "I'm not here to fight you. I

just want to know what happened."

"They escaped. The bastards stole my truck and escaped! And Rogan injected me with the serum before I could fully shift back into human form."

"*Christ.* I didn't know that could be done!"

Sean held his clothing in his hands, but there was no way he could put them on when his body was still covered with thick muscle and hair. His eyes flashed at Brett, and it was obvious his sanity was hanging on by a thread.

"Covington wants a report," Brett said.

Sean laughed, and the sound of it raised every hair on Brett's body. It was somewhere between a deep guttural growl and a human chuckle, and it just wasn't natural. He took a step back in spite of himself.

"You can tell that son of a bitch that I need more time," Sean said. "I can't go after Rogan like this, but I'll find him. I'll chase him to the ends of the Earth if I have to. He will never be able to hide from me."

"You want to tell Covington yourself?" Brett held out his cell phone.

"Don't mock me, Walker," Sean said, taking a few steps toward him. "I can still snap your neck like a twig."

"If you can catch me," Brett countered, raising an eyebrow. His skin twitched with the sudden need to shift, and he held on to that feeling while Sean stared him down. Who knew what the crazed bear would be capable of doing? If he decided to charge him, Brett needed to be prepared to shift in order to get the hell out of there.

But instead of attacking him, Sean once again chuckled. "Go back to Texas," he said. "Let a *real* shifter handle this, not some sissy pussy cat."

Brett squinted, feeling his anger rising inside of him. But he didn't lash out at Sean. Instead he smiled and bowed. "Be my guest, Sean. Seeing as how you've taken such *great pains* to take care of the problem thus far."

"Get the hell out of here, Walker!"

Brett pivoted on his heel and walked back to his Jag. Once the engine roared to life, he turned the car around and raced back down the highway, calling Covington on his cell.

"So what's the story? Where are Rogan and Wade?"

"They've escaped."

"WHAT! How is that even possible? Sean told me he had Wade. He'd captured him, for Christ's sake!"

"Sir, they stole his truck as well."

Covington was silent as Brett heard a sigh on the other end. "Is Sean that incompetent?"

"Well, Rogan was able to hit him with the serum in mid-shift, sir. I think Sean's cracking. He's not all there. He still thinks things are under control."

"Now we have no idea where the traitors are."

"That's correct. Do you want me to take care of Sean, sir?"

"No. He might be unstable, but I have no doubt in my mind that he'll eventually kill Rogan. That's all that's driving him. And personally, I can't think of a better way for that asshole Rogan to go than being on the receiving end of Sean's insanity. The real problem here is capturing Wade again. He must not be harmed."

"What should I do?"

"Catch the next flight out to Texas. We've got to regroup and see where the hell we stand. I haven't heard from Dr. Carver since I sent him back to the compound in the Rockies to see what we could salvage. He's gone MIA."

"But, if I leave Alaska, the trail will be cold. We won't know where the hell they're going."

"Do we know right now?"

"Well, no..."

"Then let Sean deal with finding them in Anchorage. I'll put in a call to the local authorities about a stolen black Hummer. In the meantime, I want you back here in Texas."

"You're the boss," Brett said, snapping his phone shut and tossing it on the passenger seat.

Twenty Two

Marlie's eyes burned as she sat in the driver's seat of the Hummer. They'd been stuck in border traffic for half an hour. For the last couple of days, they'd been driving nonstop through Canada, each of them resting in the back while taking turns driving. It was getting on toward evening, and she'd been driving all afternoon. But she wouldn't get any rest until they finally crossed the border into Washington.

They'd switched the truck's plates back in Alaska, changing their Colorado plate to an Alaskan one. Marlie had felt a momentary twinge of guilt at stealing someone's plates, but she hadn't thought long on it. They needed to be as inconspicuous as they could be in a giant black Hummer.

They'd also circled the airport in Anchorage before they left, looking for people who resembled them. Once they found a few candidates, they stole their bags, which fortunately had what they were looking for tucked inside: passports.

Just as when they'd crossed the border into Canada, Wade had once again hid in the back under a pile of blankets and pillows. Marlie and Rogan sat up front, smiling at the guard.

"Good evening," the guard said with a smile, accepting the passports Marlie had given him.

"Good evening," she replied.

"What's your business in the United States?"

"Visiting some family in Seattle," she said, hoping to God she sounded convincing.

"You bringing anything into the country? Fruit or nuts or anything like that?"

With his words, he stamped the passports and handed them back to her. He took out his flashlight and shined it into the darkened windows of the truck.

"No, sir," she said, glancing at Rogan. He winked at her, probably to bolster her courage, but her stomach roiled regardless. They'd gotten lucky at the Canadian border. She had no idea if they'd be lucky again.

"Traveling light, eh?" he said, presumably at their lack of luggage.

"Yeah," Marlie replied. "We sleep back there. It's cozy."

"I bet. All right, Mrs. Green. Welcome to the U.S."

"Thank you," she said, rolling up the window. Her skin crawled as she drove over the border.

"Stay down, Wade," Rogan said behind his hand. "We're not out of the woods yet."

Marlie continued to glance in the rearview mirror with sweaty palms, but no one was sounding an alarm. Once they were a few miles away, a sign on the road alerted them to a rest area.

"Pull in here, sweetheart," Rogan said. "I'll take over."

"Nope," came Wade's muffled voice as he finally sat up. "You drove before Marlie. It's my turn. Not that much further anyhow. I reckon I can drive us all the way to Portland. We should roll into the Rose City in about five hours. You guys get some rest."

Marlie parked the Hummer and glanced at Rogan. His eyes bored into hers, and she shivered. Cuddling with him in the back and falling asleep in his arms was exactly what she wanted to do.

"Sounds heavenly," she said.

The side of Rogan's mouth curved into a sexy grin, and he held out his hand. She took it, following him into the back of the truck. When Wade pulled the Hummer back onto the road, Rogan's arm curled around her waist as he pulled her closer.

"You all right?"

"Is that how you guys crossed the border when you came to find me?"

"Yup. Stole a couple of passports from men who kind of looked like us. Faked our way across."

"Good Lord, you guys could have been caught!"

"Made sure we crossed over the border in hats and sunglasses. The guards were none the wiser. Besides, we just crossed again doing the same trick."

"I *never* want to do that again," Marlie said, scooting closer to her husband's warm body. "That scared the crap out of me."

"Let's hope we don't have to."

"Amen to that," Marlie said with a deep sigh.

~ * ~

Rogan ran to the keypad and cursed foully. He didn't have the code to free the shifters, and he knew he had to be quick as his every move was being captured by the security cameras. After running back out to the chain-link fence where the guards were handcuffed, he grabbed one of them and shook him hard.

"Tell me the code!"

"The code is... 95325. Please... please let me go! Please!"

*Rogan didn't have time to deal with the man. He merely ran back through the gate and punched the code into the pad without another thought. A short bell could be heard just as the doors to the cells opened, releasing all the shifters in the B*E*A*S*T* compound.*

Too late, Rogan remembered the bound guards as they began screaming in agony. Glancing toward the fence, he could see the one he'd just been talking to being devoured by a lion. The other two guards were just as helpless, trying in vain to fight off a black bear, a Bengal tiger, and a leopard. Dark red blood stained the teeth of the shifters as they exacted their revenge upon the men shackled to the fence.

Jesus. Sweet Jesus! Stop…

"STOP!"

Rogan sat up, glancing around the back of the Hummer in frantic disorientation.

"Rogan?" It was Marlie. "Are you all right?"

"Christ, buddy," Wade glanced over his shoulder as he pulled the truck onto the shoulder of the highway and stopped. "What's going on?"

"I… I'm fine."

"Are you sure? You're covered in sweat." Marlie felt his forehead. "You don't have a fever."

"I told you, I'm fine. Just had a horrible dream."

"You want to talk about it?" she asked.

"No!" he exclaimed, a little harsher than he'd intended. "I'm sorry, Marlie. But no. I don't want to talk about it."

Turning on his blinker, Wade once again pulled out into traffic. "Goddamn, Wolfe. You just about scared the shit out of me."

Rogan couldn't help but chuckle. "Sorry about that," he said, lying back down with a sigh.

Marlie lay next to him, tucking his hair behind his ear. She didn't say a word, but he could see her concern in her eyes.

"After what I've been through, sweetheart," he said. "I'm bound to have a few bad dreams."

"I know. But if you ever want to talk about them—"

"You'll be the first person I come to, I promise."

"Can I ask you a question?"

"Shoot."

"When you were sleeping, I saw something on the back of your neck. It said *B*E*A*S*T* #105*. What does that mean?"

"I've got one too," Wade said. "*B*E*A*S*T* #133*. Wanna see?"

Rogan scowled at him. "Shut up and drive, Cougar."

Wade flashed him a grin and made a kissy-face in the rearview mirror.

With a sigh, Rogan turned back to his wife. "That was my number at the compound. I was experiment #105. They gave all the shifters a number. I suppose it made things easier for the scientists if they were torturing a number rather than a name."

"So, it's a tattoo then?"

"'Fraid so," he said with a nod.

"I can't believe all the horrible things they did to you. To *all* of you."

"Neither can I. Guess there are some seriously evil people in the world."

Marlie stayed quiet after that. It was a while before Rogan spoke again, but his voice was soft as he held her to him.

"Marlie?"

"Hmm?" she answered with a yawn.

"I've been wanting to ask you something for awhile now but never really had the chance until now."

"What's that?"

"Will you change your name?"

Marlie sat up to look him in the eye. "Change my name? You don't like Marlie?"

Rogan had to smile at her. She was so beautiful with her bottom lip stuck out like that.

"Sweetheart, I love your first name. I meant your last name. I want you to be Marlie Wolfe."

She sucked in her breath, and he could tell by her scent that he'd shocked her.

"Are you serious?"

He arched his brow at her. "I want you to wear my ring again, right?"

"Well… yes."

"Then I'm serious about this too. Matthew Silver doesn't exist anymore. The only man I am now is Rogan Wolfe. If you're still my wife, then your name is Wolfe now, not Silver."

Marlie stared at him for a good long time—long enough to make him wonder what her answer would be—but after a few moments of silence, she smiled at him.

"I don't care what name I wear, Rogan. As long as it's *yours*."

"I was hoping you'd say that," he murmured as he pulled her back down for a kiss. She stroked his cheeks and ran her fingers into his hair. He sighed at the feeling.

As Marlie snuggled close once more, she lifted her lips to his ear and whispered softly, "I love you, Rogan Wolfe."

She tucked her head underneath his chin and held him close. In that moment, Rogan felt as if he could conquer the world.

Twenty Three

Noah Carpenter smiled when he gazed at the woman he loved as she slept on the couch not too far away. Lanie had fallen asleep reading a book, and she looked so peaceful despite the whirlwind the past few weeks had been for both of them.

Since they'd liberated the B*E*A*S*T* compound in the Colorado Rockies, they had made their way west following the word of the B*E*A*S*T* scientist they'd met along the way who had told them of other compounds. The prospect terrified Noah, and his blood ran cold at the thought that B*E*A*S*T* was much bigger than anyone had first realized. He had no idea what he would do if they ever found a second compound in the Pacific Northwest, but they had to do something. They had to at least try.

Along with the scientist, they'd also come across a few other shifters in the mountains, limping and scared out of their minds. Once Noah and Lanie had convinced them they were the good guys, they'd banded together. The other men's names were Trevor, a lion; James, a falcon; Mac, a jaguar; Jet, a leopard; Jason, a bald eagle; and Tyler, a lynx. Six in all. They were good men, and loyal to a fault.

It had taken a lot for Noah to convince Mac not to kill the scientist when they'd first encountered him, since Mac had just recently been tortured with some particularly nasty electrical shock tests. He didn't care whether or not the scientist hated B*E*A*S*T* as much as they did. To him, the only good scientist was a dead one.

Once they'd reached Portland, Noah and Lanie had managed—thanks to her father's no-limit credit card—to rent a house that butted up to the Columbia River. God bless Richard Erickson for giving them that card. It had already been their salvation on more than one occasion.

The house itself was two stories with four bedrooms. The master bedroom was given to the scientist, because even though he was a man who had once experimented on the shifters, no one wanted the responsibility of letting him out in order for him to use the bathroom. One of the first things they did when they rented the house was go to Home Depot and buy a few sheets of plywood to board up the windows of the master bedroom. For all intents and purposes, the scientist, Luke Cooke, was in a cell. A very nice cell, but a cell nonetheless.

Each of the other shifters doubled up in the other three rooms and made sure someone guarded the door to the master bedroom at all times—despite Luke's insistence that a twenty-four-hour guard wasn't necessary.

With a sigh, Noah scooped Lanie into his arms, and she sighed with a soft smile, laying her head on his shoulder.

"My hero," she whispered.

He couldn't help but smile. "I try, my dear," he said, climbing the stairs.

"Will you come to bed with me?"

"Yeah. It's late."

"Is Tyler in our room?"

"No, tonight is his turn to guard Luke's door," Noah said, knowing exactly where her thoughts were headed.

"Maybe we can use that to our advantage, Mr. Carpenter."

"Mmm, I hope so, baby."

Just as he walked into their room and started to put her on the bed, his cell phone rang on the dresser.

"Damn," he groaned, laying his head on her shoulder. "What timing."

"Don't answer it," Lanie pleaded, bunching his shirt up his belly.

"I've got to. It's probably Rogan wanting directions. It's been a few days since he called." He walked to the dresser and grabbed his phone. "Noah here."

"Noah! Hey there, buddy. Good to hear your voice!"

"Wade! How are things?"

"Good, man. Listen, we're just about to cross the Oregon border. We've been driving literally for days—straight through without stopping. Our asses are numb, and we're going insane. Please tell me we're close."

Noah chuckled. "You're in luck. If you're near the border, then you're right on top of the Columbia River. We're renting a house on the riverfront, so it won't be too far of a drive."

"Can you give me directions? I think we're almost there."

For the next five minutes, Noah explained the directions to Wade on the phone. "Do you think you can manage?"

"Who you talking to? Of course I can manage. Pshaw!"

A wide grin spread out on Noah's face. "Can't wait to see you guys again. Hope you get here soon."

"See you in a bit."

Noah hung up and sauntered back over to his mate who was still lying on the bed.

"I take it they're almost here." she said.

He nodded, looking down at her as she raised her arms on the pillows.

"Do we have enough time to…" She let her sentence hang.

"Baby, you should know by now that I can go quick or I can go all night long. You have but to ask."

Lanie gave him a sexy grin and began pulling him down with her on the bed. "Then I want you now—hard, fast, and wild."

Noah closed his eyes and shuddered. "Dear God, woman. I'll never get used to your plain talk."

"Just shut up and kiss me, Tiger."

~ * ~

"Well, here we are!"

Wade's chipper voice cut through Marlie's skull like a knife. Her head was pounding, but she was more than thankful to finally get out of the truck and stretch her legs. Wade parked the truck in the driveway of the house Noah was renting and turned off the engine. A white Lexus they assumed was Noah's sat in front of them.

"I think that's the first time in about three and a half days that this truck has been turned off."

Rogan chuckled at him. "You forgot all the times we stopped for gas."

"Ah. Right you are. Damn, I don't know about you guys, but I'm ready to crash."

"I'm ready for other things." Rogan's gaze pierced Marlie to the core, making her blush furiously.

Wade merely chuckled, climbing out of the driver's side door. Once Wade was out of the truck, Rogan leaned closer to her and lowered his voice.

"It's been a long time, Marlie."

She knew what he meant, but she said, "Only a few days."

"An eternity."

Leaning past her, he opened the back doors of the Hummer. "I'm just letting you know that I intend on breaking this dry spell. Very soon."

Marlie bit her lip and accepted his hand as he helped her out. "I'm counting on it," she said as she playfully patted his cheek.

Once they made it to the porch, the door swung open, and Noah greeted them before they even knocked.

"Hey, guys!" he exclaimed, giving Rogan and Wade a hug and turning to give Marlie a hug as well. "I feel like I already know you," he said, grinning at her from ear to ear.

"The feeling's mutual," Marlie said with a smile for the handsome man with sandy blond hair and blue eyes. According to Rogan, Noah could shift into a white tiger. Marlie imagined those blue eyes were even more striking in a tiger's face.

"Come in, come in," Noah said. "The others are all sleeping right now, but you can meet them in the morning. We have a couple of pull-out couches you can sleep on if you're tired."

"Good," Wade said, trudging into the house wearily. "I've been driving since Canada. I wanna crash."

"Sure thing, buddy," Noah said, leading him to one of the couches in the living room.

"Where's Lanie?" Rogan asked. "I can smell her all over you."

Noah grinned devilishly. "I'm afraid I tuckered her out not too long ago. She's asleep upstairs."

"I bet she is," Rogan said with a wink, the corner of his mouth lifting. He cast a glance at Marlie and wagged his eyebrows. "You got a shower around here, Tiger?"

"Yup. Down the hall and to your left. Towels are in the cabinet above the toilet."

Rogan grabbed Marlie's hand and began pulling her down the hallway. Fortunately, her injured foot gave her no more twangs of pain as she trotted to keep up with him.

Looking over her shoulder, she waved at Noah and called out, “It was nice to meet you!”

~ * ~

Wade chuckled as he settled in between the covers and said in a sing-song voice, “I know what they’re gonna do!”

Noah grinned. “I don’t blame him. She seems like a nice woman.”

“Marlie’s great,” Wade said behind a yawn. “Rogan couldn’t have asked for a better gal.”

“I’m glad. He deserves some happiness.” After a few moments of silence, Noah turned and said, “So you guys drove straight—”

He cut off in mid-sentence with a tired grin. Wade had already fallen asleep.

Twenty Four

"Take off your clothes."

Rogan's tone left no confusion about what was on his mind. They'd just walked into the bathroom, locking the door behind them. Once he'd twisted the faucet on the tub, he turned to her with a wry grin, slowly unbuttoning his jeans. When they were pooled on the floor, he yanked his shirt up and over his head until he was naked in front of her.

"Didn't you hear me, sweetheart?" he asked, stepping closer as he reached for her.

She *had* heard him, but she'd been so wrapped up in watching him undress that she'd forgotten his request.

"I did, but I—"

She didn't get any further because Rogan grabbed the bottom of her sweater and pulled it up until it came off, then he peeled the sleeves from her arms.

"You're overdressed," he whispered in her ear, making shivers run down her spine.

As he fumbled with the button of her pants, Marlie found her courage and touched the skin of his belly. It leapt away from her fingers.

"You have cold hands!" he exclaimed with a

chuckle.

"Will you help me warm them up?"

Finally he succeeded in unfastening her pants, and he dipped his hands inside, grabbing hold of each cheek of her backside. "You know that I will," he said right before he pressed her hips against his.

Marlie gasped, having to hold on to his neck or risk falling to the floor. He didn't kiss her but rather smoothed his hands down the back of her thighs to slide her pants down her legs.

"That's better," he said.

In no time at all, the bathroom was full of steam as Rogan led her to the tub. Stepping into it, he pulled her in with him, dragging the shower curtain closed behind them. The warm water felt so good on her cool skin that Marlie closed her eyes and moaned.

"Step into the stream of water, sweetheart," Rogan whispered, gently nudging her in front of him while he grabbed the sliver of soap on the ledge of the tub.

She didn't resist. Once her skin was wet, he turned her around to get her hair wet.

"What are you doing?" she asked without opening her eyes.

"I'm going to wash you."

Marlie's eyes snapped open in shock, but before she could say another word, Rogan's soapy hands were caressing her breasts. He gave particular attention to her nipples, rubbing and lightly pinching them until they puckered in response. Now Marlie moaned for another reason. Feeling his hands sliding deliciously over her skin had her passion suddenly flaring hot inside of her.

"Like that?"

She nodded furiously and heard Rogan chuckle.

"Thought you might," he said. "How about this?"

She felt his fingers exploring between her legs,

gently stroking back and forth on her sensitive skin. “Yes.”

“Yes what, sweetheart?”

“I… I like that.”

“What if I…” Rogan didn’t finish his sentence. Instead, he continued his erotic caress while rubbing her nipple with his thumb.

“Mmm,” Marlie said, licking her lips. Without conscious thought, she was moving her hips to the rhythm of his hand. The slick soap intensified the sensation, making her circle his neck with her arms.

Rogan groaned, finally lowering his head to take her mouth. His tongue stroked hers just as his thumb stroked her nipple. Marlie’s entire body quaked at his touch. Even though water sluiced over her skin, she felt as if she were burning to a crisp.

“Rogan. Rogan,” she panted against his lips.

“What?”

“I want… I want…”

“What, baby? Tell me.”

Reaching between them, Marlie grasped his hardened flesh, stroking gently. “This. I want this.”

Rogan’s sharp intake of breath echoed throughout the small bathroom.

“Shh,” she whispered, smiling at him.

When he opened his eyes, they were golden flames flashing at her. A few days ago she would have been frightened to see his shifter side emerging, but now—tonight—it only excited her more. Rogan growled, pressing her against the wall. Luckily there was a metal hand-hold that she was able to rest her weight on.

“Open your legs,” he commanded, his voice gritty and rough.

Marlie obeyed without question. Stepping closer, Rogan grasped her hips and thrust forward, burying himself deeply within her. Marlie cried out when he pulled her head back by her hair and kissed her savagely. His thrusts were long and deep as he held on to her thighs to steady her. Marlie couldn't help the short little cries that escaped her each time he was fully sheathed, but he felt so damn good inside of her that she strained against him for the release she knew would come.

His hand was still tangled painfully in her hair and his tongue possessed her mouth with force, but she didn't care. She matched his ardor, grabbing her own handfuls of his hair and holding on tightly. When Rogan finally came, he made a sound much like a howl. Marlie didn't think long on it as he thrust sharply forward in his passion, bringing her to climax right along with him. Locking her legs behind him, she made sure he couldn't go anywhere as they leaned against the wall, panting at their exertion.

"Christ, that was good," he growled into her ear while he simultaneously thrust once more.

More shudders ripped through Marlie's body, and she continued to clutch onto him. "You… howled," she said, running her fingers through his hair.

He gave her a wicked grin and kissed the tip of her nose. "I know."

"Probably woke the whole house," she said, chuckling.

"Mmm, I hope so."

She gasped. "Why?"

"Because I want all these shifters to know you're *mine*. And right now, they'll be able to smell it."

Marlie gave him a quizzical stare.

"Mating releases heavy, thick scents that are hard to miss, sweetheart. You'll smell like me for days."

She blushed. "So they're all going to know that we…"

"Yup." He grinned from ear to ear, finally pulling away and allowing her to stand once more.

Marlie's eyes went wide. "Well, you don't have to sound so damn smug," she said, socking him in the shoulder.

"Why the hell not?" he retorted. "I want them all to be jealous."

"One thing hasn't changed about you," she said, rolling her eyes.

"Oh? And what's that?"

"You're still a man."

Rogan threw back his head and laughed.

~ * ~

Once they'd showered and crawled into the second fold-out couch in the living room, Marlie snuggled close to Rogan in the darkness. She could hear Wade's deep, even breathing from the other side of the room and had to grin.

"I'm not as tired as I thought I would be," she said.

"Me neither," Rogan replied. "But we did get some rest from the Canadian border."

"True. It'll be dawn in a couple of hours."

"Mmm-hmm." Rogan draped his arm around her shoulders and drew her close to his warmth.

Marlie sighed and hugged him tightly. "I love you," she whispered, feeling him squeeze her tighter. But he said nothing in reply.

Marlie bit the inside of her lip. After all they'd shared, she felt closer to him than ever, yet he still hadn't admitted to being in love with her. He wanted her to wear her wedding ring and change her name to Wolfe, but did he love her? Were his feelings due to some primal, possessive need to make her his mate again simply because she had once been his wife? She decided just to ask him outright.

"Rogan?"

"Yeah?" He ran his hand up and down the skin of her arm.

"Do you love me?"

He drew in a deep breath and held it for a few

seconds before expelling it. "I… I don't know."

A sharp pain stabbed through Marlie's heart. "You don't *know*?"

"Marlie, I have deep feelings for you. I know that much is true. I know I loved you long ago—I can feel it. And I remember the way you taste, every inch of you. I feel a closeness with you, Marlie, a deep bond. I want you with me, to be my mate. But… but it might be a little soon for me to say I love you for sure. Before a few days ago, you were nothing to me but a shade of a memory."

Tears filled her eyes and she tried hard not to sniffle, but she should have known Rogan could smell her change of mood.

"Damn it, Marlie," he said, turning her over to look down at her. "I didn't mean to make you cry."

"I know," she said, angrily wiping away the tears. "I had just hoped that you… that…" With a sigh, Marlie rolled over, giving Rogan her back. "Just forget it. Let's get some sleep."

"No. Now I want to talk about this."

"Why? There's nothing to talk about."

"Well, what about *you*?"

Marlie rolled over to glare at him. "What *about* me?"

"You say you love me, but do you really? Do you love me—Rogan Wolfe—or do you love the man you remember, Matthew Silver?"

"I love you. And him. I love you both!"

"Do you?"

"You know that I do. How can you say that?"

"Sweetheart, you told me that we've known each other for years. That you gave your heart and soul to me. But, Marlie, you didn't give those things to *me*. You gave them to *him*."

"But you *are* him," she cried, her tears falling into

her hair.

"Not anymore."

She sniffled before she said, "Are you sure you want me to take Wolfe as my last name?"

"Only if you're sure you love *me*, the man I am now and that I will be for the rest of my life. I'm never going to be the man you married."

Marlie tried hard not to break down into sobs at the thought that Rogan didn't love her.

"Then why are you so determined to claim me as your mate?" she asked. "Why do you want me so much if you don't love me, Rogan?"

He sighed once more. "Because you are a beautiful, passionate woman, and you're the one thing I still have that B*E*A*S*T* couldn't take away from me. I don't ever want to lose that."

Marlie was silent for a few moments before answering him.

"Being your mate means nothing to me without your love," she whispered, rolling over once more.

"Marlie…"

Rogan sighed in the darkness and touched her shoulder, making her flinch. But he didn't try to embrace her or pull her close or kiss her tears away. Instead, the springs of the mattress bounced as he rolled over as well, facing the other way. Marlie couldn't help her sniffles. She knew he could smell her sadness, but she didn't care.

Apparently, he didn't care either.

Twenty Five

Marlie couldn't sleep, and the sky was lightening with the dawn before she finally heard Rogan's breathing even out in sleep. They'd shared some incredible sex not more than a few hours before, and here she was silently lamenting her decision to stay with her husband.

Hearing him tell her he didn't love her had crushed her heart. What she'd told him back in Alaska was the truth—she loved him with everything inside of her. But his words had some truth to them as well. She couldn't believe that her husband wasn't dead and had come back to her. Accepting him for the shifter he was now seemed insignificant against the realization that he wasn't dead.

But he didn't remember her. All the memories they'd made together were gone. Rogan couldn't remember their wedding day or the day he'd climbed over the fence to impress her as a teen. That knowledge alone was enough to make Marlie sick to her stomach. He was a different man now.

The problem was that *she* could remember. She

knew every detail about him, about the man he used to be. But she had no idea who he was now. Was he right? Were her feelings for him merely an extension of her love for Matthew?

Sniffling, Marlie knew it was true. But there was absolutely no way for her to separate him in her mind. Rogan was Matthew and Matthew was Rogan. She didn't care what he'd been turned into. The fates had returned him to her. Even if he was a changed man, she could no more fall out of love with him than she could sprout wings and fly.

As soon as she had that thought, she chuckled to herself. Some of the shifters in B*E*A*S*T*'s repertoire could in fact do just that, including Rogan's good friend Justin, who'd died at the hands of Sean.

With a sigh, Marlie rose from the pull-out bed and walked to the window, glancing over her shoulder at Rogan. He seemed so peaceful lying there. Perhaps she should give him his space. She'd admitted that she loved him, but she could barely remember a time in the past few days when she hadn't been cuddled up next to him. If he didn't love her, then the last thing he needed was to be smothered by her. She'd only push him further away.

The Columbia River was calm as it rushed by the window. Marlie grabbed her shoes and slipped them on. Maybe sitting down by the water would clear her head.

The rear door of the house opened and shut without a sound. Just as the sun peeked over the horizon, Marlie made her way down by the water, sitting on the shore with her knees to her chest. She absently twirled her wedding ring around her finger and wondered if she should truly wear it on her finger as Rogan had asked her to do. He'd all but admitted that he only wanted her as some kind of trophy, a part of his past that he could still vaguely remember. But she'd told him that her marriage vows stood in her eyes and nothing had changed in that regard.

However, that didn't stop her thoughts from becoming toxic, wondering if her relationship with Rogan was ever going to turn into what it once had been. Could the same man fall in love with her twice?

~ * ~

Rogan cracked open his eyes as the sun poured through the window, hitting him directly in the face. Rolling over, he noticed the other side of the bed was empty. Marlie was gone.

"Shit," he growled under his breath.

Kicking off the covers, he bounded off the bed, following Marlie's scent until he came to the back door. He glanced out the window and saw her sitting by the water, her forehead resting on her knees. His heart wrenched inside of him.

Had she even slept? He doubted it. He knew he'd broken her heart, and he dragged his fingers through his hair painfully. The urge to shift and kill something was strong, rippling through him like an itch he couldn't scratch. He wanted to howl out his frustration; he wanted to run to her and pull her into his arms, but he knew it wouldn't be that simple.

He cared about her, that much was obvious. And he wanted her something fierce. But was that love? Could he honestly say with one hundred percent certainty that he loved her?

"Whatcha doin'?"

Wade's voice in his ear made Rogan jump. How the hell had he sneaked up behind him? *Damn, I'm losing my mind*, Rogan thought to himself.

"Ooh, never mind," Wade said. "I can see for myself. You two have a fight?"

"Not… exactly," Rogan said.

"You gonna tell me?"

"It's none of your business, you know."

"I'm going to find out one way or the other, you know," Wade countered. "Might as well tell me and save me the trouble of beating it out of you."

Rogan sighed, but he couldn't help the grin that tugged at his lips. Wade was nothing if he wasn't tenacious.

"Marlie asked me if I loved her last night."

Wade nodded nonchalantly until the words registered. Once they did, a look of horror came over his face. "What did you say?"

"I told her I didn't know."

"Oh, please tell me you didn't."

"I did."

"Oh, Wolfe. Why didn't you tell her what she wanted to hear?"

"Because I'm not going to lie to my wife." Rogan turned away to watch Marlie out the window once more.

"Why not? Husbands have been doing it for years."

"Not this one. She deserves to know the truth."

Wade was silent for a few moments before he said, "So, traveling through two countries to find her, getting shot for her, dodging Sean and making love to her, not to mention demanding that she wear her wedding ring again—those are all signs of a man who doesn't love his wife?"

Rogan exhaled the breath he hadn't realized he'd been holding. "I don't know. Christ, Wade. Quit with the third degree already!"

Wade shrugged and moved to lean on the kitchen counter not more than a few feet away. "I'm just saying it sounds like you're trying to find a reason *not* to love her."

"Why would I do that?" Rogan turned, pinning him with an angry glare.

"Oh, I don't know. Just in case Sean succeeds in killing her, maybe? You won't have any love invested in her, so you'd be able to write her off."

"You make it sound like I'm a heartless prick."

"If the paw fits…"

Rogan shook his head and growled low in his throat. "If you want to avoid a hole in your face, you'll drop this, Cougar. Right now."

"No, I don't think I will." Wade narrowed his eyes. "It's a hard truth, Wolfe, but you gotta face it before you push her away for good."

Rogan's emotions roiled inside of him. Now more than ever he wanted to shift, if only to teach Wade to mind his own friggin' business.

"If anyone's love should be questioned," Rogan said, "it should be hers."

Wade rolled his eyes. "What the hell are you talking about?"

"She told me she loves me, but how can she? She loves me because I used to be Matthew."

"True, that's probably some of it, but give the woman some credit. She of all people knows the difference between *you* and the man you *used* to be. If she says she loves you as Rogan Wolfe, then you gotta trust that and be damned thankful that she didn't reject you for being a shifter."

Pushing away from the counter, Wade stood right in front of Rogan and stared him down.

"Don't you think for one minute that I wouldn't give everything I am to trade places with you, Wolfe. You and Noah both have something I could never dream of—a woman who loves you. A woman who doesn't care if you're a shifter, a woman who's not afraid of who you are. Sure, I pretend I don't care, I pretend it doesn't bother me, but you know what? It *does.* I wake up every morning wishing I had someone to tell me they loved me. If you let Marlie slip through your fingers, then *I'm* going to put a hole in *your* face. And that's a fact."

He stormed past Rogan, swinging the back door

open wide before slamming it behind him. Rogan watched as his friend marched down to the edge of the river and squatted in the dirt to talk to Marlie. A muscle ticked in Rogan's jaw as tears stung his eyes.

"God *damn* it," he whispered to himself.

~ * ~

Marlie could hear the crunching of pebbles behind her, and she bit her lip. She wasn't going to turn around to face Rogan. She was going to keep her cool and stare out into the middle of the river.

"Hey there, Marlie. What are you doing out here?"

Relief flooded through her. It was Wade. Turning to him, she gave him a bright smile.

"I just couldn't sleep. Thought maybe I'd get some rest out here. It's not as cold here as it was in Alaska."

"You can say that again," Wade said with a chuckle. "That's a big river."

Marlie nodded. "This is the river Lewis and Clark paddled down two hundred years ago."

"Oh, yeah?"

"Yup. Saw a documentary about it. They were damned happy to finally see the ocean."

"I bet."

A few moments of silence permeated the air until Wade decided to speak up once more.

"Rogan loves you, Marlie."

Every muscle in her body tensed. "Did you hear us talking last night?"

"No," he confessed. "But Rogan's awake in there. Told me what happened."

Marlie hung her head. "He might… care for me, Wade, but it's not love. B*E*A*S*T* took that from him along with his memories."

"I don't think so."

Swallowing hard, Marlie brought her gaze up to

meet his, trying hard to keep her tears at bay.

"Before we found you," Wade went on, "he was like a man possessed trying to get to you. The thought of you with another man made his skin crawl. You wouldn't believe how many times he growled at me for even suggesting that you might have moved on after his supposed death. I think his memories of you also include the feelings of Matthew Silver, but he's too damned scared to admit that to himself."

"But why?"

"Because of what he is now. He's a man who can shift into a wolf, and he's running from another man who can shift into a grizzly. I think that deep down he believes you'll eventually reject him for who he is. Opening himself up to you fully would leave himself vulnerable to even more pain, and the man has endured more than his fair share. But he does love you, Marlie."

Tears fell down her cheeks as she pressed her forehead to her knees. "I wish I could believe that," she said, her voice muffled.

Wade rubbed her shoulder gently. "He'll tell you sooner or later. He's just stubborn as hell."

"Yeah, that's my husband for you."

Glancing at each other, they both chuckled.

"You can say that again." He grinned and looked back out over the river.

Twenty Six

It didn't take long at all before the other shifters descended the stairs. Rogan surmised that they must have been awakened by Wade's violent exit. Rogan thought they seemed eager to meet him, the story of how he'd released the shifters at the B*E*A*S*T* compound evidently having already spread throughout the household. Soon, the aroma of bacon and eggs filled the air as the man named Jet started breakfast for everyone.

"Rogan!"

Turning to look behind him, Rogan saw Lanie running down the stairs toward him. He'd barely opened his arms before he was tackled by Noah's mate, squeezing the air out of him.

"Easy, baby," Noah said, descending the stairs behind her. "You'll make Marlie jealous."

Lanie's eyes twinkled. "Ooh, Marlie! Where's your wife? I want to meet her."

Rogan opened his mouth to speak, but before he could, he heard Marlie's gentle voice behind him.

"I'm right here."

Turning to look at her, he saw her standing near the

back door with Wade, and he could tell she was avoiding his eyes.

Lanie walked over to her, holding out her hand. "It's so nice to finally meet you. I'm Noah's mate, Lanie Erickson."

Marlie took her hand with a smile. "I'm Marlie Sil—Wolfe. Marlie Wolfe."

Her use of his last name wasn't lost on Rogan, and his eyes widened. She'd just used his name! Perhaps she really did care about him. But he didn't have long to think on it before Noah was talking again.

"Well, I don't know about you guys, but I'm starving!" he exclaimed, clapping Rogan on the shoulder as he eased into the kitchen. Looking over Jet's shoulder, he said, "So… what's the ETA?"

"About five minutes."

"Good. Any longer than that, and I'm risking an ulcer."

Rogan watched out of the corner of his eye as one of the shifters introduced himself to Marlie.

"My name is Jason," he said with a grin.

"Marlie," she replied, shaking his hand politely.

The man was taking too long to pull away, and Rogan growled as he walked over to them. "The name's Rogan," he said, stepping between them. "I see you've met my *wife*."

Jason nodded and chuckled. "Indeed I did. You're a lucky man."

Looking behind him, Rogan caught Marlie's eye. "Yes, I am."

"*Breakfast*!" Noah's loud bellow echoed throughout the house. "Who's gonna take Luke's plate?"

"Who's Luke?" Rogan asked.

"Our scientist friend."

"I'll do it," Rogan said, holding out his hand for the

plate. "I knew a lot of B*E*A*S*T*'s scientists when I worked with Tam. I want to meet this guy."

Noah shrugged. "Be my guest."

~ * ~

When Rogan reached the top of the stairs, he came face to face with the shifter guarding the door to the master bedroom.

"Oh, thank God," the man said with a wide grin. "I thought I was going to die from hunger. You must be Rogan."

"That's right."

"Name's Tyler. Nice to finally meet you. I've heard so much."

Rogan grinned. "Go on down. There's plenty of food for everyone. I'll watch this guy for a little while."

"Thanks!" Tyler said, bounding down the steps.

Once he was out of sight, Rogan knocked on the door and called out, "Breakfast!"

"Come in."

Testing the knob, Rogan found it unlocked and opened the door. The room was dark because the plywood on the windows didn't let in too much sunlight. A small lamp was lit as a man sat on an unmade, king-sized bed reading a book.

"Ah, wonderful. I could smell the bacon and my mouth was watering."

Once Rogan got a good look at the man's bespectacled face, his blood ran cold. This wasn't just some random scientist from B*E*A*S*T* sitting before him—it was *Dr. Lucian Carver*, the very man who'd given Tam his orders to kill Noah at any cost.

"Jesus Christ," Rogan whispered, amazed that he hadn't dropped the plate in his hand.

"Not quite, Rogan," Lucian said with a smirk, putting the book down on his lap. "I was wondering if I'd finally meet up with someone I knew from the agency."

"What the hell are you doing here?"

"Can't you see? I'm reading."

"You know what I mean." Rogan's eyes flashed, and he could feel his skin itching. It was all he could do to hold back the wolf that wanted to emerge and rip out Lucian's throat.

"Well, I couldn't just let a bunch of rogue shifters kill me in the Colorado wilderness, now could I? I had to think of some kind of story they would believe."

"You son of a bitch. How can you sit there so damn smug, knowing exactly what you put these men through?"

"What you don't seem to understand, Rogan, is the fact that I created *you*. I created *them*. I created every shifter at B*E*A*S*T*, therefore I am your God, if you will. All I need to do is bide my time and the tide will turn."

"God my ass!" Rogan exclaimed, throwing the plate of food against the wall so hard it shattered into pieces. "What the hell is preventing me from shifting right now and killing you where you sit?"

"I don't know. What *is* preventing you?"

Rogan knew the man was taunting him. Every nerve ending in his body prickled—screaming, pleading, demanding that he shift and end Lucian's pathetic life. But the same doubt that had prevented him from killing Sean held him back now. He was not a killer. He hadn't let B*E*A*S*T* turn him into one, and he'd be damned if he would turn himself into one.

"I'm not like you," Rogan spat, stepping closer to the bed. "I'm not a killer."

"Oh, I beg to differ," Lucian said, taking off his glasses and cleaning them on the edge of the bed sheet.

The man wasn't even breaking a sweat, and Rogan realized his scent was calm as well. He wasn't intimidated in the least.

"You've killed plenty of times, Rogan. You just don't want to remember it."

"You're lying."

"No, I'm not. We pitted you against Sean, and that's the fight we let you remember. But there were others, Rogan. Other fights that you don't remember because we wiped them from your memory. Oh, you're a killer all right, Wolfe. Cold-blooded and ruthless."

Tears blurred Rogan's vision as his temper rose. "You're a liar."

"Am I? Can you prove it?"

Rogan ran both hands through his hair. He couldn't. There was no way he could refute Lucian's words. Thinking back to his time with B*E*A*S*T*, he couldn't remember a damn thing that would lend proof to what he'd just been told.

"No," he finally said through gritted teeth.

Lucian chuckled. "So much hate inside of you. You're trembling with it, aren't you? But I know something you don't know, Number 105."

"What's that?" Rogan asked, taking another step forward. One more step and he'd be able to pounce on the scientist and end this right here and now.

"When we brainwashed you—all of you—we implanted a safe word within your brain. All I have to do is utter it, and you'll be in a catatonic state. And you can't do a damned thing about it. Why do you think I'm not afraid of any of you? I could have escaped whenever I wanted."

The tears in Rogan's eyes finally spilled over as the implication of what Lucian had just said hit him like a ton of bricks. "Then why didn't you escape, you bastard?"

"Who could pass up the opportunity to reunite the three shifters who infiltrated and destroyed the B*E*A*S*T* compound? I have you all under one roof now. All I have to do is say the word, and I could kill you all myself."

"I dare you to do it, old man," Rogan said, feeling cocky despite the situation. "I think you're bluffing."

Lucian grinned. It was the last thing Rogan remembered.

Twenty Seven

Lucian chuckled to himself. The wolf stood stock still, staring straight ahead with his eyes glazed over. Lucian couldn't help but pat himself on the back for a job well done. The safe word had been his idea, and the proof that it still worked was standing right in front of him.

Of course, Covington had no idea Lucian had programmed the shifters with a safe word. Lucian wasn't so ignorant that he didn't know Covington planned to pull the research out from under him once the final tests had been made. The senator wanted the shifters to be America's new defense system, capable of infiltrating enemy countries and assassinating leaders and politicians as he saw fit.

But Lucian had a different vision for the shifters of B*E*A*S*T*. Bank robbers. Bodyguards. Terrorists. Assassins. Any agenda he could think of could be carried out with the monsters Lucian himself had created. Covington dreamed of ultimate power and ruling through fear. Lucian's dream wasn't nearly as ambitious, but he did see a bright and wealthy future ahead of him. Imagine what other countries would pay for the shifters! The possibilities were endless.

No, Covington could never know about the safe

word. If he ever found out, he'd do away with Lucian in a heartbeat. Even when the compound in Colorado had been falling down around his ears, Lucian hadn't used his ace in the hole so as to keep it a secret from Covington. Revealing it would have put Lucian's life in much more danger than it was in from the shifters.

And actually, the coup in Colorado had actually helped his cause. Ever since, Covington had been preoccupied with finding and eliminating the escaped shifters before things got out of hand, and that meant Lucian would be able to take over the other three compounds without Clive Covington even noticing. Lucian looked forward to the day when he could wrestle the agency from Covington's grasp—with an army of loyal shifters behind him.

But for now, he needed to call Covington and let him know where he was. The old man was probably pissed beyond measure, and now was not the time to enact his plan anyway. Lucian needed to play along awhile longer, until the time was right.

He dug his hand into the pocket of Rogan's jeans. Once his fingers brushed Rogan's cell phone, he pulled it out and grinned from ear to ear as he flipped it open. He dialed Covington's number and listened while it rang once, then twice.

"Covington," came the irritated voice on the other end.

"Clive, you will not believe where I am or who I've got with me," Lucian said, still grinning.

"Carver? Is that you?"

"Indeed it is."

"Where the hell have you been? I've been trying to get in touch with you for weeks. Do you know the kind of money I've wasted trying to find you?"

"I'm sorry I couldn't contact you before now, but

my plan has finally come full circle."

"What the hell are you talking about?"

"I've got them, Clive. All three of them. Together under one roof."

Silence answered him. Then, "You have ALL of them?"

"Yes!" Lucian scratched the top of his head as he paced, pushing his round glasses back up his nose. "Rogan, Noah, and Wade."

Covington began to laugh. "Christ, Carver. Where are you?"

"Portland."

"Oregon?"

"Right on the Columbia River. I can even give you directions."

"Excellent. Carver, I don't want you to do a thing, just get the hell out of there. I'm going to send Sean to deal with them. You hear me?"

"Loud and clear."

"I knew you wouldn't disappoint me."

"Does this mean I get a raise?"

Covington chuckled humorlessly into the phone. "That's up to Sean."

~ * ~

Sean was livid. He'd scoured Anchorage high and low for the past few days, and still no sign of the damned traitors. Their trail hadn't just turned cold, it had frozen solid.

"Shit!" he yelled, tossing the television in his motel room to the floor. He tried hard to get a rein on his raging emotions. If he didn't find Rogan soon, Covington was going to have *him* killed, no doubt about it. Then he would be on the run from that asshole.

Sean hadn't gotten any sleep the night before, choosing instead to see if Rogan and his ilk were emerging at nighttime to throw him off the scent. Still there was nothing—no leads, no black Hummer, nothing that could possibly lead Sean to them. They must have left the city.

After the serum had worn off a few days ago, Sean had been able to return to his human form and dress quickly just as a car had approached him on Glenn Highway. After flagging down the car, he'd posed as a stranded motorist until the driver had emerged from his car, then he'd killed the man, satiating his growling belly with the warm, delicate meat of the man's bowels. Even thinking of it now had his stomach rumbling. More and more it seemed as if normal food didn't satisfy him. He wanted to eat fresh, raw meat. As often as he could.

Once he'd eaten his fill, he'd climbed into the car and driven to the city of Anchorage not too far away, getting himself a motel room and frustrating the shit out of himself. Why couldn't he find that damned wolf?

Sean's cell phone rang, and the LCD panel told him it was Covington. With a sigh, he contemplated letting it go to voicemail, but he knew that'd only piss off the old man even more. And he didn't need any more heat on his tail.

Flipping the phone open, he merely uttered, "Yeah?"

"Sean, get your ass on the next flight out to Portland."

That shocked the shit out of him. "What for?"

"Have you wondered why you can't find Rogan in Alaska?" Covington asked sarcastically. "It's because he and Wade fled to Portland, Oregon when you weren't looking. So get on a damned plane and don't fail me this time. Do you have a pen?"

Sean's mind raced. Portland? The bastard had fled to *Portland*? What the bloody hell? Stumbling to the end table by the bed, Sean grabbed a pen and ripped off the back cover of the nearby phone book.

"Okay, I have a pen."

"They're in a house right on the Columbia River..."

As Sean wrote down the directions, he wondered how in God's name Covington had gotten his intel, but he didn't question it. Once he hung up the phone, he marched out of the motel room and didn't look back.

He had a score to settle, and it was high time he settled it once and for all.

Twenty Eight

When Rogan came to, he was standing in the middle of an empty room. The loud shriek of the smoke detector pierced his ears, and he had to cover them for fear of going deaf. What the hell just happened? His brain was so foggy he couldn't quite get his bearings. He'd been talking to someone… but who?

The scent of something burning wafted to him, and he raced out of the room to see the hallway filled with white smoke. Bounding down the stairs, Rogan was greeted by a strange scene. Every single shifter was frozen—some standing, others sitting, but all of them doing absolutely nothing but staring straight ahead.

The smoke was coming from the bacon burning on the stove. Rogan dashed into the kitchen, pushing a frozen Jet out of the way to dump the bacon into the sink. Once Jet hit the counter on the other side of the kitchen, he came to his senses, covering his own ears.

"What the hell happened?" he shouted.

"I don't know, but go stop that damned noise!" Rogan looked around frantically for his wife. She wasn't in the kitchen or the dining room, but once he rounded the couch to the living room, he found both Marlie and Lanie, out cold on the floor. A small pool of dried blood was underneath Marlie's head.

"Marlie!" he shouted, grabbing her shoulders and shaking her. "Marlie, sweetheart. Can you hear me?"

She moaned, and her eyes fluttered just as the smoke detector stopped it's shrieking. The other shifters began to come to at that moment, and Noah stumbled out of his chair.

"Lanie?" he called out.

"She's over here, Tiger," Rogan said, pulling his wife into his arms.

"Shit! Lanie, are you all right?" Noah dropped to his knees beside Rogan. "What happened?"

"I don't know," Rogan said, inspecting Marlie's head.

She groaned but opened her eyes and whispered, "Rogan?"

"Are you all right? Are you hurt?"

"My head… aches." She reached up with her hand, but Rogan stopped her.

"Don't touch it, honey. You've got a gash. I'll have to see if you need stitches."

"Are you all right?" she asked, her face grimacing with pain.

Rogan's heart twisted inside of him. *She* was the one wounded and still she asked about him. "Yeah, I'm fine, Marlie. I'm fine if you are."

He pulled her close and hugged her, kissing the top of her head gently. He shuddered to think what he would have done if she'd really been hurt.

"What happened?" she asked.

Rogan looked at Noah cradling Lanie in much the same way. She seemed to have a headache as well but was none the worse for wear. Suddenly, Rogan remembered the last thing that had happened before he'd blanked out.

"Noah, you're not going to believe this," he said.

"What?"

"The man you had upstairs—the scientist. His name's not Luke. It's Lucian—Dr. Lucian Carver. He was the man who gave Tam his orders to kill you."

"What the f—?" Noah's eyes flashed, and Rogan could smell his sudden anger. "I'm going to kill him!"

He moved as if to stand, but Rogan's hand on his arm stopped him. "Won't do you any good to go up there. He's gone."

"Gone? What do you mean *gone*?"

"I mean he's gone, Noah!" Rogan exclaimed. "I went in there to give him his breakfast, and I recognized him. Then he began spouting stories about some kind of 'safe word' he could utter that would make the shifters go into a catatonic state. I think from what we just witnessed, he was telling me the truth."

"Holy shit!"

"It gets worse," Rogan went on. "His plan was to get us all under one roof again. He's escaped, and my hunch is he's alerted the big wigs behind B*E*A*S*T* as to where we are."

Marlie clutched Rogan's shirt with a vengeance. "You mean we've got to run again?"

He glanced at her and his gaze softened. "I don't know what else to do."

"Is it ever going to end?" she asked.

"Not as long as the bad guys are after us." He felt her shiver in his arms. "But for now, we're going to get you looked after. You got a first aid kit around here, Tiger?"

"In the bathroom." Noah replied.

Rogan scooped Marlie into his arms and walked with her down the hall.

"My head is spinning," she said.

"I know," he whispered, lowering her to sit on the

lid of the toilet. "That bastard probably hit you with something to knock you out since the safe word wouldn't have worked on you and Lanie. Do you remember anything?"

Marlie shook her head then sucked in her breath between her teeth at the motion. "No. Just a blinding pain and then darkness."

With a sigh, Rogan pulled out the alcohol and cotton balls. "This is going to sting, sweetheart." She cried out at the first contact of the alcohol on her scalp, and he said, "I don't think you'll need stitches. Just be careful when you brush your hair."

When he was done cleaning her wound, he could smell her change of mood and knelt in front of her, taking her hands in his.

"I'm so tired of crying," she whispered. "I'm so scared, Rogan. What are we going to do?"

Looking into her eyes, he tucked her hair behind her ears. "We're going to get the hell out of here. We're going to go somewhere where they can't find us."

"Where is that, Rogan? Where can we possibly go?"

"I don't know," he answered truthfully.

With a sob, Marlie collapsed in his embrace. His arms curled around her, and held her tightly. Her sweet scent surrounded him and he breathed it in.

"That man could have killed you, Rogan," she whispered in his ear. "I don't ever want to…"

"To what?"

Marlie pulled away from him, staring at her hands in her lap. She shook her head and got up. She would have moved around him to walk out the door, but his large frame stopped her.

"Marlie, what's wrong?"

She sniffled but still didn't meet his eyes. "I don't… I don't want you to be… to feel smothered by me."

Rogan just stood there, speechless.

"I'm sorry if I've… made you uncomfortable by clinging to you," she said.

"Marlie, what are you talking about?"

She lifted her eyes, and he could finally see all of her hurt, all of her pain. It broke his heart.

"I'll give you all the space you need," she said. "I don't want you to feel forced into… caring for me."

"But I do care for you," he said, framing her face with his hands.

She smiled gently with quivering lips as her tears spilled over. Giving him a small nod, she patted his hand and said, "I know you do."

She squeezed past him and walked back down the hall. Leaning on the counter after she'd gone, Rogan stared at himself in the mirror and had never felt more alone than he did at that moment. The look in her eyes had reached inside of him and grabbed hold of his heart with a vengeance. She loved him. He'd bet his life on it. And she believed he cared for her and that was all. But was it?

Growling at his own reflection, Rogan tried hard to get a grip on his own emotions. He had no goddamned idea whether or not he truly loved his wife, but seeing her pain was killing him inside.

Was love *supposed* to hurt so damn much?

Twenty Nine

"So, what do we do?" Wade asked.

Marlie trembled as she watched the men talking in the living room. Her head was still pounding, and she had to sit down at the dining room table. Lanie was sitting next to her, biting her nails.

No matter what she did, Marlie couldn't stop shaking. She couldn't remember how she'd fallen unconscious to the floor, and that scared her most of all. The scientist, Dr. Carver, could have killed her if he'd wanted to.

"I don't know," Rogan answered Wade. "We'll have to leave."

"And go where?" Mac, the tall, imposing shifter, paced back and forth. "Where the hell are we going to go? They know every move we make!"

"I don't know, but we can't stay here." Rogan sighed loudly. "Look, I have no doubt that Sean's been alerted to our presence. He'll come for me—for all of us. And he's a crazy son of a bitch. He's literally insane."

Trevor, a handsome man with sandy blond hair and dark eyes, decided to speak up. "I say we hole up here. Stay and fight. Send those assholes back to hell."

A few of the other shifters nodded in agreement.

"If we stay here," Noah pointed out, "then we're *all* in danger. Especially the women. They can't defend themselves like we can."

"Then send them away," Mac said with a growl.

"No!" Lanie exclaimed, standing from her chair at the table. "You're *not* sending me anywhere. I agreed to go with Noah wherever he had to go, and that includes fighting B*E*A*S*T* if we have to."

All eyes turned to the dining room, and Marlie blushed when Rogan's eyes rested on her, but she didn't say anything.

"Sending them away isn't a bad idea," Rogan said.

Marlie's heart fell, and she glanced at Lanie who arched a brow at her. Marlie stood up. "I'm not leaving my husband."

Mac shook his head. "You women are crazy. Do you know what B*E*A*S*T* will do to you if they catch you?"

"Of course we know!" Lanie said with her hands on her hips. "Marlie and I aren't so fickle as to toss our men aside when the going gets tough."

Noah snickered behind his hand.

"Damn, Tiger," James said with a chuckle. "You have a feisty one."

"That he does," Rogan agreed with a grin on his face.

Marlie had no idea why he was suddenly smiling, but she couldn't help the smile she gave him in return.

Mac growled. "If they stay, they need to keep out of our way. We can't afford to have them in the middle of this."

Rogan held up his hands. "Wait, wait, wait. We haven't even decided yet if we're going to stay here and fight."

"Maybe we should," Wade piped up. "We have a chance here to find out who's behind it all. And if Sean's who they're sending, well… why don't we set a trap for him? I know he's got a cell phone. Imagine the numbers he's got in his speed dial. We can find out who these bastards are and take the fight to them."

"Wade's right," Jet said with a nod. He had to snap his head back to get his black hair out of his eyes. "They're not going to stop until we take a stand. We have *nine* shifters here. We're a small army."

Everyone nodded and James said, "You're right, Jet."

"We don't even know if they're only sending Sean," Rogan said. "They could be sending an army of their own as well. And what if Sean knows this safe word?" Rogan glanced at each man. "What then?"

"You think the agency would tell their safe word to one of the most unstable shifters they've got?" Noah said. "I'd be willing to lay money down that he doesn't even know there *is* a word."

Rogan nodded. "Good point." Looking back over his shoulder, he once again pinned Marlie with his handsome gaze. "You sure you ladies want to stay?"

"Yes," Lanie said with a firm nod.

Marlie nodded as well. "Yes, I do."

"Then that settles it," Rogan said. "We stay and face whatever the hell those bastards can throw at us."

"What about that story Luk—I mean Lucian—told us about the other B*E*A*S*T* compound?" Trevor asked. "Is that just a fairy tale?"

"Probably," Noah said, rolling his eyes. "We can't take a damn thing that man said as gospel. He's been lying to us since day one."

"I knew I should have ripped out his throat when I had the chance," Mac said, baring his teeth.

"Well, we can't totally write off the possibility of another B*E*A*S*T* facility," Jason said as he plopped down on a nearby couch. "It's altogether possible that it really exists out there."

"Damned if we do, damned if we don't," Rogan muttered. "Well, there is one thing we have on our side."

"What's that?" Tyler wanted to know.

"Wade and I stole Sean's truck back in Alaska. We have a few guns, including a tranq gun."

"Excellent," Noah said, rubbing his hands together. "Then let's go get armed."

~ * ~

"You scared?" Lanie's voice broke through Marlie's thoughts as they sat on the couch together.

The men were crowded around the dining room table plotting out their trap for Sean. Their excited voices carried throughout the house, and Marlie knew they weren't paying attention to her conversation with Lanie.

"Shitless," she replied, chuckling nervously.

Lanie smiled and placed her hand on Marlie's knee. "These men won't let anything happen to either of us—especially Noah and Rogan. They have too much invested in us."

"Noah, maybe," Marlie said under her breath.

Lanie arched her brow. "Is something wrong between you and Rogan? Want to talk about it?"

Did she? Marlie didn't really know Lanie at all. On one hand, she didn't feel comfortable talking to her about something so personal, but then Lanie was the only one who would possibly be able to understand where she was coming from.

With a shrug, she said, "He just…"

"What?"

"He doesn't love me."

Lanie scoffed. "Who told you that?"

"He did."

Her eyes went wide. "Well, damn. That *is* a

problem."

"I feel like he only came to find me in Alaska to find out more about himself. Wade says Rogan *does* love me, and when we're together, I… I can't believe that he *doesn't*. He's so tender and gentle. I'm just so confused."

"What did he say *exactly*?" Lanie asked, scooting closer to Marlie on the couch to keep her voice down.

"I asked him if he loved me."

"And?"

"And he said he didn't know."

Lanie clucked her tongue. "Well, that's inconclusive."

Marlie grinned. "You're telling me."

"But he didn't come right out and say no, so that's a good thing."

"Is it? I wanted him to say yes."

Lanie sighed. "Give him some time. The man was tortured at B*E*A*S*T*, then he found out he had a wife and has just gotten back together with you. I think he's a little confused himself."

"He wanted me to wear my wedding ring again. And he also asked me to change my name from Silver to Wolfe."

"Well, there's your proof right there. He does love you."

"How can you be so sure?" Marlie asked.

Lanie smiled. "Because men are stupid. They hear the word *love,* and they run for the hills. But his actions speak louder than his words. You say he's tender and gentle. He wants you to honor your wedding vows to him and even change your name for him—again. Did he ask you to be his mate?"

Marlie blushed furiously as she stared at her folded hands. "He didn't ask."

Lanie gasped. "He didn't?"

"No, he…"

"What? You've gotta tell me now!"

"He *told* me I was his mate. I didn't have a choice in the matter."

Lanie giggled. "Oh, honey. He's got it bad."

"You think?" Marlie felt her heart lifting a little.

Lanie nodded enthusiastically. "Rogan's in love with you, Marlie. Probably madly in love. He just doesn't know it yet."

"So what do I do until he realizes it?" Marlie glanced over her shoulder at Rogan. He was so handsome sitting there at the table with the others, his fingers steepled in front of his face.

"Live like he's already told you," Lanie said. "Don't push him away—that will only confuse him even more. The more loved he feels, the more he'll fall head over heels for you. Trust me."

Marlie smiled as she watched her husband. As if he sensed he was being watched, he glanced over at her, catching her eye. His slow smile took her breath away.

"See?" Lanie whispered. "There's your proof. When that man looks at you, nothing else in the world exists for him."

Lanie was right. The look in his eyes told Marlie exactly what she needed to know. Rogan did love her. When his eyes flashed gold at her, giving her a glimpse of the wolf inside him, her heart skipped a beat. His eyes only flashed for two reasons—when he was angry, and when he wanted her.

And Marlie was quite certain that Rogan wasn't angry at the moment. She blushed a deep crimson as she held his eye contact, but she didn't look away.

Neither did he.

Thirty

Sean pulled his rental car up to the curb and smiled. There, in the driveway of the house he'd come all this way to find, was his black Hummer.

It had taken him a good eight hours to get to Portland from Anchorage. He'd had to wait a couple of hours before departing because there was a layover in Seattle, and the flight had been delayed. The flight itself had taken only about five and a half hours—the layover only about forty-five minutes. Getting the rental car had been a hassle, and he'd been a hairsbreadth away from shifting and killing someone, but he had to be patient—he knew that. Killing Rogan and his wife would be worth the wait.

By the time he'd followed Covington's directions and pulled up to the house, it was nighttime and his belly was growling. A wolf and his mate were on the menu, and Sean couldn't help the chuckle that escaped him. Perhaps he should eat Marlie in front of Rogan. But there was more than one way to eat *her*.

Sean's belly revolted at the thought of doing anything with Marlie that didn't involve feasting on her warm blood, but watching Rogan scream and cry while Sean violated his wife would be sweet music indeed. And he wanted to make that wolf howl before he was through with him.

Then he'd kill Marlie right in front of him. He'd tear her flesh to ribbons while her delicate bones crunched in his mouth. Saliva dripped from his lips and he had to wipe it away with the back of his hand. Maybe he'd kill her first *then* violate her still-warm corpse. Mmm, yes, that would be delicious. Sean got hard just thinking about it.

Once he opened the car door, he knew for sure this was the right house. He could smell the bastard Rogan mingled with other tantalizing scents. Wade and Noah were here as well, along with a few other smells that were unfamiliar. No matter. Whatever was behind that door, Sean had no doubts that he could handle it. One way or the other, he was going to get the better of Rogan Wolfe.

Now. Here. Tonight.

~ * ~

Marlie couldn't stop shivering as she sat upstairs with Lanie in the room she and Noah shared with Tyler. The men had insisted they keep the door locked no matter what they heard beyond it. Marlie swallowed hard, knowing full well that the door wasn't going to stop Sean if he really wanted to get to them. Just in case that happened, Rogan had left her with her grandfather's shotgun.

The men had a plan, and she prayed it would work. James had made a trip out to the nearest store that sold camping supplies and had bought a can of bear repellant, along with some thick coils of rope. Having lived in Alaska where bears were prevalent, Marlie knew the repellant existed. Her father had been an avid hunter, and he'd never failed to carry the stuff whenever he went into the Alaskan wilderness, but it was really nothing more than glorified pepper spray, guaranteed to stop a bear in its tracks—exactly what they needed.

But their plan didn't appeal much to Marlie, because Rogan was their bait. The others knew Sean would be able to smell them if they hid inside the house, therefore they'd found various hiding spots outside the house—all upwind, of course—in order to be ready for Sean when he arrived. Rogan was the only one who was going to be waiting for him inside, sitting in the middle of the living room with nothing but the bear repellant and the tranquilizer gun. Noah and Wade had the two rifles that had been in Sean's truck and were the closest to the house, just in case something went wrong. But they all wanted the grizzly alive.

Waiting for Sean had to be the most nerve-racking time of Marlie's life. The long minutes ticked by, each one seeming as if it were an eternity. The minutes joined together, and hours passed until the sun finally set. She began to wonder if he was truly going to come or if they were just being paranoid.

Marlie glanced out the window when she heard the sound of a car door slam. There on the street stood Sean, looking as if he was sniffing the air. Her heart leapt into her throat, and her fear almost choked her.

"Oh, God," she moaned under her breath, her skin prickling.

"What?" Lanie asked, moving to look out the window herself.

"He's here."

~ * ~

Rogan sat on the couch, ignoring his body's demand to shift. He knew Sean was there—Tyler had rapped on the back door twice to alert Rogan to his presence. It was impossible to stay calm when he knew the bastard was right outside, probably plotting his own trap.

On second thought, Rogan seriously doubted that Sean had any kind of plan. He had never been one to think things through. He merely rushed into things, blindly hoping his brawn could save him from whatever lay ahead.

Marlie was upstairs, and Rogan hoped she was clutching the shotgun he'd given her. If anything went wrong, he didn't want Sean getting his claws into her. She knew to run and run hard if she had to, but Rogan wondered if she would. She and Lanie both seemed determined to stay with the shifters, come what may. It both impressed him and annoyed him at the same time. Now that Sean had arrived, there was no hope of sending the women away somewhere safe, and it was probably just as well. Rogan knew both he and Noah would have never heard the end of it if they'd made the women leave.

The front door of the house suddenly splintered as Sean slammed against it once, then twice—rocking the entire house on its foundations. The door finally gave way on Sean's third attempt, and he stepped over the threshold, growling with a grin on his face. It didn't take long for him to see Rogan on the couch, probably because his scent would have permeated the room by now.

"There you are, you sneaky bastard," Sean said, licking his teeth. "Where's your pretty wife?"

"That's none of your concern, Sean," Rogan said coolly, still sitting and holding on to the repellant with a vengeance. "You came here to finish this, Grizzly. So let's finish it."

"That's where you're wrong," Sean said with a chuckle. "I came here to torture you, Wolfe." He took a deep breath as he glanced up the stairs. "And that's exactly what I'm going to do."

With a speed Rogan didn't even know he possessed, Sean sprang up the staircase. For a split-second, Rogan couldn't believe his eyes. Sean was going after Marlie!

"*Shit!* He wants Marlie!" he shouted desperately to the others outside before he sprinted up the stairs after Sean.

~ * ~

Wade's ears caught Rogan's desperate cry, and he cursed foully.

"Sean's after Marlie! Let's go!"

"Christ, Lanie's with her!" Noah exclaimed.

"Remember, we don't want to kill him!" Jet yelled as they began to run toward the house.

"If that grizzly lays one hand my mate," Noah yelled back, "I don't make any goddamn promises!" With that, he charged through the ruined front door.

~ * ~

The door to the bedroom imploded, and Marlie screamed at the top of her lungs. Sean stared at her as if she were his next meal, and she had no doubt that was what he was thinking when he wiped his mouth with the back of his hand.

"Hello there, little lady," he said, sauntering into the room. "Fancy us meeting again."

Marlie raised the barrel of the shotgun, trembling so violently that she had trouble keeping it steady.

"Shoot him!" Lanie yelled, hiding behind her.

"They want to keep him alive!" Marlie said.

"Screw that! Kill the bastard!"

Before Marlie could even cock the hammer, Sean pounced, ripping the gun out of her hands so fast that she squealed in disbelief. He tossed it behind him and lunged for her. At that same moment, Rogan ran into the room and jumped on top of Sean's back, curling his arm around his neck in a choke hold.

"You're not going to lay a finger on my wife!" he growled into Sean's ear.

Sean tried to unseat Rogan a few times, but to no avail. His face was turning redder by the second, but that didn't stop him from changing his body right in front of them, shifting into the giant Kodiak he could become and tearing out of his clothing. Rogan could no longer hold on to his massive neck, and with one shake from Sean, he went flying across the room. The bear turned to attack him as he lay prone on the floor.

Marlie could see the can of bear repellant Rogan must have dropped in the struggle. Picking it up, she yelled at Sean.

"Hey, you ugly bastard! If it's me you want, come and get me!"

"Marlie, what the *hell* are you doing?" Lanie yelled, backing into the corner.

Sean turned to look at her, growling and snarling as foam dripped from his jaws. Marlie's heart was beating a mile a minute, but she stood her ground, terrified beyond her wits. Grasping the can of spray with her right hand, she brought it up just as Sean moved toward her and sprayed the bear fully in the face.

She watched as he shrieked in pain. Again and again he swiped his paws in his face, as if desperate to rub the sting from his eyes. It didn't take long before the other shifters appeared in the doorway, Noah and Wade leveling their rifles at Sean.

"Wait!" Rogan shouted, crawling on all fours to reach the tranquilizer gun he'd dropped in the fray. But just as he grabbed it, the massive bear knocked him over and straddled him on the floor.

"ROGAN!" Marlie cried out, her tears streaming down her face. Sheer terror entered her heart when she realized she was about to lose her husband—again. "Rogan, *no!*"

The loud crack of a gun shot rang through the room, and Sean's bellows became sluggish as his large head bowed closer and closer to Rogan on the floor. The bear slowly shifted, his body distorting and changing shape back into Sean, whose entire face was red and puffy from the repellant.

"I'm going to… kill you… you fu—"

With that, Sean collapsed on top of Rogan, who immediately kicked him off. Marlie's heart resumed beating when she saw the tranquilizer dart sticking out of Sean's belly.

"Someone inject him. Now!" Rogan commanded, standing from the floor.

Jet ran in with a syringe of serum and stuck Sean in the neck. Once that was done, the others clambered into the room and dragged him away, intent on carrying out phase two of their plan.

Noah crossed the room and grabbed Lanie in a swift hug, kissing her like there was no tomorrow. Marlie looked at them then glanced at Rogan, who crossed the room in much the same way. Grabbing her arm none too gently, he crushed her to him, lowering his mouth to hers and tasting deeply. Marlie could barely keep up with his onslaught, but she clutched onto him fervently, knowing full well the extent of his relief.

"I could have lost you," he whispered to her once he released her lips.

"Rogan, you scared the shit out of me," Marlie said, making him chuckle.

"I was just about to say the same thing to you," he said, giving her another kiss.

"That didn't happen quite the way you'd planned, did it?"

Rogan shook his head. "No. Sean came after you instead. Didn't see that one coming."

Sniffling, Marlie laid her head on his chest and listened to his galloping heartbeat. "Why do you think he came after me instead of you?" she asked in a small voice.

"He wants to make me suffer, sweetheart. He wants to kill you while I watch."

"Jesus," she whispered.

"You said it."

“Do you think your ropes will hold him?”

“We’ve given him the serum, which means he won’t be able to shift for another four hours. We have enough doses to hit him eight more times if we need to. So that’s about thirty-six hours right there.”

“What happens if he manages to escape?” she asked.

Rogan swallowed hard before answering. “Then we’re gonna have to kill him.”

Thirty One

"Make sure his bonds are tight," Rogan ordered. "I don't want this son of a bitch breaking free."

He watched as Mac, Jet, and Tyler bound an unconscious Sean to a chair. Not only were his wrists tied behind the back of the chair, a length of rope also went around his chest and arms, holding him upright. Another strip of rope was tied around his thighs, holding him to the seat, while a third piece of rope secured his ankles to the legs of the chair.

"How long is he going to be out?" Jason asked as he stood next to Rogan and watched the others tie him up.

"I don't know. Another hour at least. But he won't be able to shift."

"Look what I found!" Wade exclaimed as he came downstairs with a pile of Sean's ruined clothing.

"What?"

"His cell phone."

Wade held it up in his hand to show everyone as he grinned from ear to ear. He flipped it open but frowned after a few minutes.

"What's wrong?" Rogan asked, stepping close to

look over his shoulder.

"Sean doesn't have anyone in his speed dial. Damn it!"

"Try his call history," Noah said, attempting to fix what was left of the front door.

"Ooh, good idea."

Marlie padded over to Rogan and, without a word, gently took his hand. He glanced down at her and squeezed but didn't say anything either. She smiled at him.

"Clive Covington," Wade said suddenly.

"Clive who?" Jet asked.

"Covington. That's who he's been calling. He doesn't call anyone else."

"Weird."

"Spoke to him just today—right around the time our scientist friend decided to do his disappearing act."

"No shit?" Rogan said, raising his brow. "Then this Covington must be the guy—like *THE* guy. If we find out where this man is, we might be able to take the fight to him."

Noah gave up on the door and propped it up against the wall before wandering back over to them in the dining room, scratching his head. "Clive Covington? Now why does that name ring a bell?"

"You've heard of this guy?" Wade asked, holding up the phone.

"Yeah, somewhere. I don't know where though."

"Maybe you heard his name at the B*E*A*S*T* agency," Rogan said. "If he was a bigwig there, it's possible we might have heard his name from the scientists talking amongst themselves."

"I guess," Noah said. "But it seems to me it was from something much more recent. I don't know."

"I should call him," Wade said.

"Don't be an idiot, Cougar." Rogan scowled at him. "We don't even know who he is or why Sean's been talking to him. Just wait until after we've interrogated Sean."

Wade growled but snapped the phone shut. Stuffing it into his pocket, he said, "Fine. I'll wait. But until then, you guys got a computer?"

"Um, yeah," Noah replied. "This house came fully decked out, equipped with a computer, Internet and everything." He led Wade down the hall to the family room.

"Do you think Sean's going to tell us what we want to know?" Marlie asked Rogan in her timid voice, staring at Sean and still clutching Rogan's hand.

"I don't know, honey," he said, draping his arm around her shoulders and pulling her close. "But there's too much at stake here not to at least try and get some answers out of him."

"What are we going to do when we run out of serum?" she wanted to know.

Rogan shuddered. "I've got no goddamn idea."

~ * ~

Wade hadn't even been sitting at the computer for a full minute before chills ran up and down his spine. After opening up an Internet browser, he'd searched for Clive Covington. What he found made his blood run cold.

"Rogan! Noah!" he yelled, standing from his chair so fast that it fell over.

Within moments, both of them rushed into the room. "What is it, Wade?" Rogan asked with his eyes wide.

"Jesus, you're not going to believe who this man is!" Wade exclaimed, pointing at the computer screen and backing away as if it were a poisonous snake.

Noah leaned over the desk to look at the monitor and gasped himself.

"What?" Rogan asked again.

Noah straightened and stared at him. "Covington is a United States senator. From Texas."

Rogan's eyes went wide as he looked at Wade, who

was biting his lip. A *senator*? He could hardly believe what he'd just read. Covington was not only a senator, but apparently he had his eye on the White House for the upcoming elections in November.

"Oh my God," Noah whispered, reading further. "I know why this man's name was so familiar to me. I saw him on the news the other night! Lanie and I were watching a little TV, and he was on the news, smiling and shaking people's hands. I think he donated money to some hospital or something."

"*This* is the man behind B*E*A*S*T*?" Rogan said, glancing back and forth between Noah and Wade. "A *senator* who wants to become president? Holy shit, what if he wins the election in November? Christ!" He paced back and forth, running his hands through his hair brutally.

Wade growled low in the back of his throat. "He won't if I have anything to do with it."

"Now, Wade," Rogan said with a sigh. "We can't go doing anything rash."

"Rash? *RASH?"* Wade looked incredulous. "Rogan, for God's sake, he made us into freaks! Monsters! We can *NOT* let this man win his bid for the White House."

"So what are you proposing we do?"

"Get all the information out of Sean that we can, then find Covington and end this once and for all."

"It's not going to be that easy, Wade," Rogan said. "We *know* Sean isn't the only one in the picture. Brett's a part of this too. God only knows how many shifters this man has behind him. Not to mention tight security."

A suffocating anger rose up within Wade. He balled his hands into fists in order to resist shifting and racing to Texas right then to rip out the bastard's throat. Who did Covington think he was, playing God with men's DNA?

Wade had been tortured to within an inch of his life while he'd been inside the walls of the B*E*A*S*T* compound. He wasn't about to sit idly by and let this asshole—this MONSTER—get away with what he'd done.

"I don't know what we're going to do," Wade said, his voice low. "But we've *got* to do something."

~ * ~

Rogan smiled as Sean came to, his head bobbing this way and that on his shoulders. They'd moved him to the garage to get him out of the house and also to interrogate him. Rogan knew things might get a little nasty. After the scare Marlie had gotten already, Rogan wasn't about to put her through any more grief. It would only upset her more.

Armed with two syringes—one of the serum, the other of tranquilizer—both Noah and Wade held their rifles aimed at Sean's chest. Rogan brought another chair out to the garage, seating it just a few feet away from him. He straddled it, crossing his arms over the back of the chair and laying his chin on his arms.

Once Sean was fully conscious, he looked up and saw Rogan. Immediately, he began snarling and yanking on his bonds.

"Won't do you any good," Rogan said with a grin. "We tied you tight, my friend."

"I am *NOT* your friend!" Sean spat the words in his face.

Rogan wiped his eyes. "Well, that's an understatement." He gave Sean a damning glare. "We want to know who you work for."

Sean chuckled. "You think I'm going to just give you that information?"

Wade walked up and twirled his gun in his hands a moment before cracking Sean on the side of the head with the butt of the rifle.

"Yeah, that's what we had in mind," he said.

Sean looked dazed a second before shaking it off. "Do you think that by giving me the serum that any of you saved your own lives? I'm going to kill you all one by one, and delight in eating your remains."

"If you don't mind me pointing it out," Rogan said with a cocky grin, "it looks like *we* have the upper hand here, not you."

"I'm not telling you a damned thing!" Sean snapped. "You can torture me all you want. I've suffered worse at the hands of B*E*A*S*T*."

"Oh, I don't doubt it," Rogan said, nodding his head. "But you see, you went after my wife. And no one threatens Marlie and gets away with it."

"You're a pussy, Wolfe. Always have been. That's why you couldn't kill me in Alaska. You don't have it in you to be a killer."

"Is that what you think?"

"That's what I *know*."

"Dr. Lucian Carver seems to think different. He told me about a few fights I'd been involved in before the one with you—fights they didn't let me remember. He said I was a most efficient killer."

Sean's face visibly paled. "When did you talk to Carver?"

"Does it matter?"

Narrowing his eyes, Sean said, "You're lying."

Rogan shook his head. "I'm afraid not. You can't tell me you ran upstairs and didn't smell the bastard. Oh, he was here. And he had a few things to say."

Sean just growled in reply.

"Maybe they called off our fight because they knew I would win," Rogan said, enjoying the chance to taunt him.

Sean's growl became a snarl.

"Maybe they knew I wouldn't be merciful; that I'd rip you apart," Rogan said, arching a brow.

Sean thrashed in the chair.

The side of Rogan's mouth lifted in a sneer of his

own. He'd definitely hit a chord. He'd had a sneaking suspicion about why Sean Ross hated him so much, and now it was confirmed. The man couldn't stand the thought that he'd lost their fight and that the scientists had ended it to save his life.

"How do you know it wasn't the other way around, Wolfe?" Sean yelled. "How do you know they didn't stop the fight because they were worried for *you*?"

"Because *I* wasn't the one bleeding."

Sean tried hard to break free until the business end of Noah's rifle suddenly lifted his chin, making him rethink his actions.

"Why don't you calm down a bit, hmm?" Noah said, pressing the barrel into Sean's neck.

Sean glared up at him but said nothing as he foamed at the mouth.

"Let's try this again," Rogan said, once again resting his chin against his arms on the back of the chair. "Who is Clive Covington?"

Sean's eyes flashed for a moment but said nothing. Noah cocked his rifle, and the sound of it echoed in the empty garage.

"Nobody," Sean finally said.

"Hmm, that's funny," Wade said, his voice laced with sarcasm. "Because your cell phone says you called *nobody* about twenty-five times."

With a growl, Sean stared straight at Rogan. "I'm going to kill your wife. I'm going to kill her and feast on her remains. Then I'm going to find a hole and fu—"

The butt of Wade's gun once again cracked against the side of Sean's skull. "You gotta focus here, big guy," Wade whispered into his ear. "Who is Covington?"

Rogan fidgeted in his seat. Hearing Sean talking so brutally about Marlie made his skin crawl. He knew Sean would be able to smell his annoyed scent, but there was no helping it. And hearing exactly what Sean had planned for Marlie didn't sit well with him. His protective, possessive emotions were coming into play.

"She's going to taste so good, Wolfe," Sean went on. "I'm going to eat her. And then I'm going to *EAT* her."

This time it was Noah who cracked him in the head. Sean spit blood onto the concrete floor.

"You are a psychotic son of a bitch." Rogan growled and stood up, then he bent over to be right in Sean's face. "You can't stand the fact that I'm better than you. You can't stand the thought of knowing that I would have killed you in that ring so long ago. It burns inside of you, doesn't it? Festering like the plague, eating at your heart until all you can see is your own revenge. You don't even care how you get it, do you? As long as you kill Rogan Wolfe. As long as you come out victorious. Will that make you feel more like a man, Grizzly? Will killing Marlie compensate for the fact that you can't possibly be half the man that I am?"

"Killing your wife will give me the satisfaction of watching you become nothing more than a broken shell of a man," Sean said, spitting blood into Rogan's face.

Rogan calmly wiped it off and stood up straight. With a nod, he said, "Makes sense. That's the only way you could win a fight against me, isn't it?"

Sean suddenly roared, fighting against his bonds like a man possessed.

"You should give up now, Grizzly," Rogan said, stepping further away. "I've already bested you twice. Once in Alaska and once here."

Wade shook his head. "Nope, Wolfe, you got that wrong. You've bested him *three* times."

"Oh, is it three?" Rogan pondered, tapping his chin.

"Yup. You're forgetting your pit fight at the B*E*A*S*T* compound."

"Oh, that's right! Make that three times."

"Bastard!" Sean screamed. "I'm going to kill—"

Rogan spun on Sean and punched him square in the jaw, releasing all his strength as a shifter upon the unsuspecting man. Sean's chair toppled and he hit the ground hard.

"I've heard all that before!" Rogan yelled at him. "Can't you come up with anything *new*?"

Sean was seething. Rogan could see it in his eyes, but he was beyond caring. The bastard had crossed so many lines that Rogan was a hair away from killing him there on the floor.

"We know who Covington is, Sean," he growled as he bent down to look into his eyes. "He's a senator from Texas, isn't he? Thinks he can get into the White House and create some kind of super army. For what? The War on Terror?"

Sean didn't say a word. He merely lay there, breathing heavily with his lip dripping blood.

"It doesn't matter, you know," Rogan whispered with a grin. "We're going to stop him one way or the other. That man won't even get to *knock* on the front door of the White House."

Sean began to chuckle at his words. "You're a fool, Rogan," he said through his laughter. "Covington will kill you before you even know what happened!"

Rogan nodded. "Oh, you mean like now? He sent *you* to kill me, and look where we are." Glancing around him, he spread his arms wide, indicating the bare garage.

"If you don't kill me, Wolfe," Sean sneered, "then I'm going to kill you. AND her."

"You've said that before," Rogan said, scratching his head. "I guess you leave me no choice in the matter, do you?"

Nodding at Noah, Rogan watched as he jabbed the syringe of tranquilizer into Sean's arm.

"What the hell are you doing?" Sean cried, writhing on the floor. Within a few moments, he was once again out like a light.

"Holy *shit*, Rogan," Wade said, lowering his rifle. "This bastard's not going to tell us anything. All he can see is his hatred for you."

"I know."

"He's never going to stop hunting you," Noah said, running his fingers through his hair.

"I know that too."

"Well, what the hell are we going to do with him?" Wade asked, throwing his hands into the air.

"That I don't know." With a deep sigh, Rogan spun on his heel and walked back into the house.

Thirty Two

"I won't be able to sleep," Marlie said as she sat with Rogan on the couch. He was staring off into space with his arm draped around her shoulders.

"Hmm?" he asked, finally looking at her.

"I said I won't be able to sleep. Not with Sean so close."

"Me neither," Rogan said, giving her a squeeze. "At least *you* can't smell him."

"Oh, God. Yeah, I'm glad I can't."

Rogan chuckled.

"I'm so scared," she said.

"I know. But we have three shifters in there guarding Sean. He can't untie himself, and he won't be able to shift for awhile. For now, he's harmless."

"Who's guarding him?"

"Jason, James, and Tyler."

"Oh, good. I thought maybe Noah was in there too, but Lanie was so scared after you took Sean down. She needs Noah right now."

Rogan smiled as he stroked her arm. "I'm sure he's upstairs comforting her."

Marlie went silent, wishing Rogan would comfort her in the same way. Though she tried hard not to think about it, she knew he could always smell her change of mood, and now was no exception.

"We have almost no privacy here, sweetheart."

"I know," she said softly, turning into his chest.

The silence in the house—aside from Wade's deep, even breathing on the other pull-out couch—was almost deafening. It was late, and the shifters who weren't guarding Sean were sleeping.

"Wanna come out to the truck with me?" Rogan asked, lifting Marlie's chin to look into his eyes.

"The truck?"

"Yeah. We'll be able to have some time together, just me and you. And I won't be able to smell Sean."

Marlie gave him a smile. "I'd like that."

Rogan stood and grabbed her hand. "Come on," he said, swiping the truck's keys from the kitchen counter.

The front door had been jury-rigged to get it to stand in its frame. Rogan and Marlie carefully opened it and made their way outside hand-in-hand. Once they got to the truck, Rogan unlocked the back doors and they both climbed inside.

"There," Rogan whispered in the darkness once the doors were shut behind them. "This is much better."

Marlie blushed when his palm caressed her cheek. She could barely see more of him than a shadow in the darkness, but she knew he could probably see her as clear as day. She didn't touch him, but she wanted to. She wanted to dip her hands under his shirt and caress the soft skin of his belly. She wanted to lean into his lips and kiss him, but she also didn't want to push her feelings onto him, regardless of the passion they'd shared in the past few days.

"Marlie?" Rogan's deep voice startled her, and she jumped.

With a nervous chuckle, she said, “What?”

“I realized something today.”

“Hmm?” She turned her face into his hand, kissing his palm.

“When Sean broke into the house and went after you, I’ve never been so scared in my entire life. Not even when I was faced with my own death at the hands of B*E*A*S*T*. That fear of losing you almost choked me. I was desperate to save you, sweetheart.”

Marlie licked her lips and brought her hand up to take his. “I felt that fear too. I was terrified Sean was going to rip you to shreds.”

Rogan scooted closer to her, making the Hummer rock slightly. “I think for the first time, I knew some of what you’d gone through when you thought I died two years ago.”

Bringing her eyes up to his, she held his gaze.

“How on Earth did you survive?” he whispered.

Marlie could feel the tears behind her eyes, and she didn’t try to stop them. Perhaps confessing to Rogan exactly what she’d done after his death would be a way of healing the wounds in her heart.

“I lived one day at a time,” she said. “There were days when I didn’t think I *would* survive. You were my entire world, Rogan. I was so naïve. I had no idea how the world worked beyond my vet clinic. You were always my rock, the one I could turn to, the one who would know the answers to anything. When I lost you, I was lost myself. I… visited your grave every single day. I couldn’t take this ring off no matter how hard I tried. And even though men would look at me, I just couldn’t move on. My family urged me to get rid of your clothes and your pictures. I guess they thought if I erased you from my life, it would be easier for me to bear. They were even shocked when I decided to stay in that house. But I kept all your clothing, and I kept all your photographs. At least once a week, I would dig through them and have a good cry. I would even go through your old clothes and smell them, although your scent had long since vanished."

She paused and put a hand on his face.

"Having you come back to me has been like a dream—a dream come true. Even though I know you're not the same man I married, it's more like you are and you aren't. I want you to know, Rogan, that even though I mourned deeply for Matthew, I know and accept that he's gone. When I say that I love you, I mean that I love *Rogan Wolfe*, the man my husband became. I'm sorry if I hurt you before when I told you that being your mate meant nothing to me. I was lying, Rogan. It means the world to me. And I'll stay with you even if… even if…"

"Even if what, honey?" he whispered when she trailed off.

She shook her head. "It's enough that I love you, Rogan. I have enough love inside of me for the both of us."

Rogan hung his head and sighed. "Marlie, I'm sorry for hurting you the way I did. It's taken me a while to realize it, sweetheart, but… I *do* love you. I think I never *stopped* loving you. Even when I was being tortured at the hands of B*E*A*S*T*, I remembered you and found solace in my memories. It's true that Matthew Silver no longer exists inside of me, but he *did* leave one thing behind—his love for you. God, Marlie, when Sean went after you, I knew then that I loved you. I couldn't lose you. I couldn't—"

He didn't get any further, because Marlie grabbed his face with her hands and pulled him to her, kissing him fervently. He didn't fight her. Instead, he pushed her down onto the bed of the truck, bringing his knee between her legs.

"Rogan," she whispered against his lips. "I love you. I love you so much!"

He surged against her, invading her mouth with his hot tongue. "I love you too, Marlie. Christ, how could I doubt it?"

He kissed her once more, and Marlie gave in to her desires. Pulling his shirt out of the waistband of his jeans, she ran her hands up his belly, threading through his coarse hair. Rogan groaned in response, releasing her mouth to gaze at her. His eyes flashed a bright gold, and Marlie smiled.

"Wolves mate for life," she whispered as she unbuttoned his jeans.

"Yes, they do," he said, nodding with a grin as he fumbled with her jeans as well.

"I'm never going to leave you."

"I'm never going to *let* you leave."

Marlie chuckled at that. "Then make love to me, Wolfe," she demanded.

"Woman, I thought you'd never ask."

Thirty Three

She smelled divine. After the horrid stench of Sean that permeated the house, Marlie's passionate scent was driving Rogan wild. Her eager hands unbuttoned his jeans, slipping under his waistband and into his briefs, and he gasped at her touch.

"What are you doing, sweetheart?" His voice sounded deep and ragged, even to his own ears.

"I want to love you," she answered, kissing the side of his neck. "Every inch of you."

Her hands clasped around his erection, making him gasp again and squeeze his eyes shut. He knew Marlie had no idea what she was doing to him. His animal side howled in his head, demanding that he satiate his desire there and then by plunging deeply into her heat, but Rogan refused to be so selfish. This woman loved him, and she deserved so much more than a quick lay.

"Marlie, let *me* love *you*," he said, laying his forehead on hers and hoping she could read his expression. If her hands continued to stroke him like they were, he wouldn't last long. But damn, he couldn't resist a few wicked thrusts of his hips to push himself deeper into her palms.

She smiled at him. "I don't think so. Not this time."

His eyes widened, wondering at the meaning of her words, but her scent said nothing about being angry or upset.

"Then—"

"Rogan," she said, "you got to taste *me* back in Alaska. Now I want to taste you."

His entire body trembled at her words. He was surprised his arms could still hold his weight. Shocked couldn't even begin to explain the feelings pulsing through him, along with his raging desire.

"Christ, woman," he hissed through his teeth.

"Roll over," she said, pushing on him and scooting out from underneath his body. Marlie still held on to him, stroking and caressing him with ungodly skill. She slowly worked his jeans down his legs, and Rogan kicked them off, frantic to give her access to him. He could think of nothing that he'd rather have her do than put her mouth on him right then.

Marlie didn't even bother undressing before she attacked him, crouching between his legs and taking him inside her mouth. They both groaned, and Rogan lifted his hips, wordlessly asking for more. Marlie's mouth was hot as she drew him in then pulled him out, slowly yet with ardor, again and again. She cupped him in her hands, and he thought he'd come at that alone.

"Do you know I used to do this to you before you were taken by B*E*A*S*T*?" she asked him in a husky voice, continuing to lick him with her slick tongue.

"God, I don't doubt it. You're friggin' good at it." Holy shit, was he seeing stars?

"You like this?" She took him in until he could feel the back of her throat.

He didn't say anything. If he did, it would be all over. And for the life of him, he didn't want this to be over—not yet. Instead, he threaded his fingers through her hair and groaned.

"I remember licking this scar," Marlie whispered, suddenly shifting her weight to his thigh.

He felt her hot tongue make its way up his leg, right where he'd injured himself on the barbed wire fence, trying to impress her as a teen. Rogan cried out at the sensation.

"Marlie! Dear God…"

She chuckled and returned her mouth to his length. "Do you know how much I love feeling you inside of me, Rogan?"

That was his last straw. Rogan sat up and pulled her forward before falling back to the floor of the truck with Marlie completely on top of him. He kissed her deeply, thrusting his tongue into her mouth and holding on to her so hard that he knew she couldn't possibly get away.

"Take off your pants, Marlie. Take them off or *Christ*, I'm gonna burst."

They had already been unbuttoned by Rogan's own hands, but she needed help taking them off while straddling him. He was glad to oblige, and soon she was sprawled across him, naked from the waist down, just as he was. He helped her to once again swing her leg over him, but before he knew what she was doing, he was suddenly inside of her, deeply rooted to the hilt. Rogan growled.

"You're so hot," he whispered, pulling her down for a few kisses. "You're so hot—and so wet. For me. My mate. My beautiful mate, Marlie."

Grabbing her hips, Rogan lifted her up only to bring her back down, making her bite her lip. He could smell her pleasure coming off of her in waves. What she'd spoken out loud was the truth—she did love having him inside of her. It made him want to roll her onto her back to drive into her savagely, but he resisted.

Marlie had asked to love him. This was her tempo,

not his. Each time she sheathed him, Rogan's control wore thinner. She was taking it slow, apparently savoring the feelings within her, but it wasn't long before she collapsed on his chest, kissing him without reserve. Her rhythm increased and Rogan moaned, answering her thrusts with thrusts of his own.

Marlie cried out, and he could feel her muscles tighten around him as she came apart in his arms. That was all it took for his own pleasure to release. With a few more deep plunges, he exploded into her, holding her hips down to his, making sure every last inch of him was rooted within her. When the waves of ecstasy passed, Rogan caressed Marlie's cheeks only to find them wet with tears.

"Marlie? What's the matter, sweetheart?" he asked, holding her close.

She sniffled but answered him. "That was just so beautiful, Rogan." Glancing up into his eyes, she whispered, "You fell in love with me. Again."

He smiled at her, wiping her tears away. "How could I not? You're a beautiful woman, and you love me so damn unconditionally. I knew I couldn't lose you—not now, not ever. Never doubt it, babe. I love you."

Marlie kissed his cheek and made her way down his neck where she buried her face and hugged him tightly. He hugged her right back and reveled in the knowledge that he was still embedded in her depths.

After a few moments of silence, Marlie's muffled voice came to him.

"Rogan?"

"Yeah?" he asked, stroking her hair.

"What will happen if I get pregnant?"

Rogan took a deep breath. *Damn*. He should have told her he was sterile a long time ago. That B*E*A*S*T* had gelded all of their experiments, apparently to avoid the chance that they'd reproduce, since no one knew what the child of a shifter would become. The thought was too horrifying.

"I… I can't have children, honey."

Marlie sniffled once more but lifted her face to look at him. "What?"

"I'm sterile. I found that out on B*E*A*S*T*'s computer at the same time I found out about you."

"Jesus, Rogan," she said, her eyes once again filling with tears as she stroked his cheeks. "What the hell did they *do* to you?"

For the first time in as long as he could remember, Rogan felt tears sting his eyes. The look she was giving him was too much to take.

"I don't remember some things, and I wish I could forget the things I do remember. Marlie, I need you to keep me from going insane. If I think about what they did to me for too long, I get overwhelmed. I don't know how to deal with it."

Marlie threaded her fingers through his hair, and it calmed him. He closed his eyes and sighed.

"I'm always here for you," she said. "You don't have to do it alone anymore."

Rogan shuddered as he held her close. Neither one of them said another word. It was enough for him to sit in silence, knowing that Marlie's love was the best damned thing that had ever happened to him.

He was a lucky bastard. Because he'd won her love—twice.

~ * ~

Sean awoke to find himself still tied to the chair. Shaking his head a few times, he tried to clear the fog from his brain. He could smell others with him in the garage, and squinting his eyes, he tried to make them out. None of them had the familiar stink of Rogan, so he must have returned to the house. He finally determined there were three shifters there with him, each of them with their eyes closed. What the hell were they doing?

Two of them were sitting slumped in two other chairs, while one was sitting on the floor, propped up against the wall. Sean's eyes burned and his limbs were sore. He tried to move his hands, but his circulation was so poor that he couldn't even feel them. Clearing his throat, he glanced at all three men and raised a brow. Were they sleeping?

He made another noise in his chair, but none of them stirred or even spared him a glance. Sean smiled to himself. But how the hell was he going to get out of this damned chair? That bastard Rogan had given him the serum a little while ago along with the tranquilizer. How long had it been? Sean had no idea because he'd been out the entire time. If these morons were the ones Rogan had picked to guard him, perhaps having them fall asleep would work in his favor.

Exactly how long had it been since he'd been given the serum? Sean decided to test it. Concentrating on shifting, Sean could feel the familiar euphoria of his body changing, growing thick muscle and hair. He smiled to himself as he slowly shifted. It had been longer than four hours since he'd had his last shot. These idiots had probably slept through the time when they needed to inject him again. It couldn't be *this* easy, could it?

He would have to be ready. These ropes had no hope of holding down a Kodiak grizzly, but the sound of them popping would most definitely wake the sleeping shifters. Once he shifted, he'd have to kill them all. That was the only way.

With his decision made, Sean allowed his body to fully shift into a bear. The ropes snapped like ribbons, and as soon as the shifter against the wall opened his eyes, he was dead as Sean ripped out his throat, shaking him back and forth until his neck snapped.

"Holy shit!" one of the other men cried out, but

those were his last words as Sean leapt at him, pushing him to the floor and crushing the man's chest with his massive weight.

Hearing the man's final breath filled Sean with an immense pleasure as he turned his sights on the last man. He made a dash for the door leading into the house but didn't quite make it before Sean blocked his way. The man shifted into a falcon and took flight, but he had nowhere to go.

Sean stood on his hind legs and swiped his enormous paw into the air, hitting the bird and slamming him into the far wall. The bear charged as the bird fluttered on the ground, shrieking in terror. But Sean had no mercy. With one sickening crunch, he bit the bird's head clean off and swallowed it whole. *Too damned easy,* he thought to himself.

Despite the metallic tang of blood in the air, Sean could smell the faint scent of Rogan wafting through the garage door. Was he outside nearby? He sniffed at the door going into the house then sniffed under the garage door. Rogan's scent was mixed with Marlie's, and they were definitely not in the house. Looking around for what he wanted, Sean finally found the button that would open the garage.

Fortunately, killing his guards hadn't been too noisy, so he doubted there'd be anyone to stop him before he ripped Rogan's body apart. Sean lumbered to the button and pushed it with his snout. He watched as the door slowly lifted, revealing the black Hummer in the driveway, right behind Noah's white Lexus. Sean was sure that's where the lovebirds were—he could smell their stink. They'd mated once again.

No matter. They wouldn't even see him coming.

Thirty Four

Marlie squealed as a colossal crash woke her from a satisfying sleep. She'd been resting her head on Rogan's shoulder, but once the crash rocked the Hummer, Rogan sat up, disoriented. They'd both gotten dressed after their lovemaking because it was chilly out in the truck, but neither one had wanted to wander back into the house. They'd pulled out the blankets and pillows from the side compartments and snuggled up to enjoy their private night together.

But now something was crashing into the truck—hard. Marlie's heart was suddenly in her throat.

"Jesus *Christ*!" Rogan exclaimed, glancing out the window.

"What? What is it, Rogan?" Marlie yelled.

"It's Sean! He's escaped, and he's shifted too!"

"Oh, God… oh, God…" Marlie was unable to stop the tears of terror from forming in her eyes. "What are we going to do, Rogan? What are we going to do?"

"I don't know, honey. We don't have any weapons with us."

"Shit!" Marlie's hands shook, but that didn't stop

her from opening a few of the compartments to check for herself.

Another crash rocked the truck from side to side so violently that it almost tipped.

"He's ramming us! Jesus!" Rogan turned to Marlie and grabbed her shoulders. "Marlie, listen to me. I've got to go out there and draw him away from you. I want you to run into the house and get Noah and Wade. They have the rifles. We have to kill Sean. There's no other choice."

"No!" Marlie said through her tears. "Rogan, he'll kill *you*!"

Another crash hit the Hummer, and Marlie screamed at the top of her lungs, holding out her arms as if she alone could keep the truck from tipping over.

"Babe, he'll kill us both if I stay in here! The house is a few yards away, and you'll have to sprint to get there. I want you to promise me you'll get Noah and Wade!"

Marlie couldn't speak. She was panicking and could barely breathe. Rogan grabbed her cheeks and made her look at him.

"Listen to me," he said. "Go to the house. Don't worry about me. I can hold my own against that bastard—I've done it before. You get yourself to safety." Giving her a swift, hard kiss, he said, "I love you, Marlie. Now go get the others!"

With that, he opened the back door of the Hummer and shifted at the same time, ripping out of his clothing before his paws even touched the ground. Once he was out of the truck and running up the road, Sean charged in hot pursuit, leaving her behind in the truck.

Marlie sat there and stared after her husband in shock.

"Rogan!" she cried out, not believing her own eyes. Sobbing her heart out, Marlie climbed out of the truck and ran to the front door of the house, screaming for Noah and

Wade.

~ * ~

Rogan's paws crunched through the light snow on the ground. It was nothing compared to the deep Alaskan snow, but it was still cold regardless. He didn't know where the hell he was going, but he could hear that damned bear behind him, practically breathing down his neck.

But that's when his keen ears heard Marlie behind him, yelling for Noah and Wade. Glancing over his shoulder, he saw for himself when Sean stopped short and looked back at Marlie as she ran toward the house from the truck.

Sean didn't even hesitate. Without looking at Rogan again, he turned around and charged the other way, clearly intent now on Marlie rather than on the wolf before him.

Rogan's entire being cried out for Marlie to hurry and get to safety before it was too late, but the bear's long strides were gaining on her. Then she suddenly stumbled and fell in the snow. Without knowing what else to do, Rogan tipped his head back and howled at the top of his lungs right before he took off running, determined to keep that goddamn grizzly away from his wife. Once and for all.

~ * ~

Wade woke up to a strange noise. It sounded like a… garage door opener. Sitting up from his blankets, he could suddenly smell blood in the air, and he could also hear deep growling from beyond the door into the garage. Every hair on his body stood on end, and he leapt from the pull-out bed. He grabbed his pants and tugged them on before yelling up the staircase and banging on the wall.

"*NOAH!* I think Sean's escaped!"

Glancing around the darkened living room, Wade found his rifle and made sure it was loaded. He grabbed the extra ammo magazine on the side table near the couch and stuffed it into his pants. He didn't wait for Noah, he merely yanked open the door to the garage and almost puked at the wave of blood that hit his nostrils. Jason, James, and Tyler were all dead! Holy shit!

At that moment, Wade heard Marlie screaming in the front yard just as Rogan's distinctive howl rent the air. Wade dashed to the driveway only to see Sean charging Marlie who'd stumbled in the snow. She was sobbing and trying like mad to get to her feet and make it to the front door before Sean caught her.

With his adrenaline pumping, Wade aimed and fired his rifle, catching Sean in the shoulder. The bear stumbled and went down, giving Marlie the time she needed to make it to the front door just as Noah crashed through it, holding his own rifle trained on the bear.

With a roar, Sean stood once more and ran toward Wade just as he fired and missed. Another gunshot cracked through the air as Noah fired, hitting the bear in the flank. Sean released a mighty howl but continued his charge. Wade lifted his gun once more, but he was too late. Sean's gigantic paw swiped the gun aside, and he pounced on Wade, both of them tumbling in the snow.

Wade didn't even think, he merely shifted as fast as he could and growled as he sank his sharp teeth into Sean's neck. The mighty bear stood and shook Wade off. The cougar landed a few feet away, dazed.

Sean stood over him, and Wade was sure it was the last thing he was ever going to see. But at that moment, Rogan jumped on the grizzly's back, sinking his fangs into his thick hide. Sean roared once again, trying to shake Rogan off, but he was unsuccessful. Wade could see Noah aiming his rifle, but he didn't shoot, probably for fear of hitting Rogan.

Standing up from the snow, Wade lunged once again, ripping at Sean's face with his sharp claws. But he'd underestimated the bear's strength—even with multiple bullets in his flesh. Sean swiped his claws, hitting Wade right in the soft flesh of his belly. Blood poured on the ground as Wade yowled in pain, his pristine golden coat stained red. The pain was so intense that he could do nothing more than lie on the ground in stunned disbelief.

~ * ~

Rogan was too pissed to care about Wade at the moment. He wanted Sean dead and, at this point, he'd stop at nothing to do it. With a mighty heave, Sean finally managed to unseat him, and Rogan went rolling in the snow. But he wasn't down for long before he stood once more, springing past the grizzly as it lumbered toward him.

Sean's paw caught nothing but air as Rogan leapt over it. The bear screamed, his hot breath puffing white in the cool midnight air. Rogan tore past him once more, taking a bite out of Sean's flank as he passed. With a growl, Sean stood on his hind legs and roared, presumably to intimidate him. Rogan would have chuckled at Sean's lame attempt at getting the upper hand if a wolf could laugh. The bear was bleeding badly, thick pools of blood already littering the ground.

With a quick glimpse at the house, Rogan noticed that Noah had run out to grab Wade, pulling him from the fray. Good. He didn't want his friend to get hurt any more than he already was. Once Sean came down from his hind legs, Rogan launched himself at him once more, yelping as Sean succeeded in batting him out of the air. Rogan hit the ground so hard that the wind was knocked out of him. The world spun in circles, and he yelled at himself inside his head to get up or Sean would kill him.

Rogan managed to regain his footing, but he wasn't quite stable. Once again, he smelled Marlie's sweet scent on the wind and groaned when he saw Sean chuffing at the air as well. Sparing another glance at the house, Rogan could see Marlie outside on the lawn. What in God's name was that crazy woman doing?

Son of a bitch!

~ * ~

Marlie screamed when Sean clawed Wade in the belly right before her eyes. The cougar went down, panting hard in the snow. Rogan was trying desperately to get the bear away from him, and he succeeded long enough for Noah to run out onto the lawn to grab Wade by the scruff of his neck and pull him to safety.

But when she heard her husband yelp, Marlie was desperate to help him. A few yards away near the driveway, she saw where Wade had dropped his rifle. If she could just get to it, she might be able to take down that bear.

Before Marlie could move, Lanie put her hand on her shoulder, somehow knowing her thoughts. "You go out there and you'll get yourself killed!"

"If I don't," Marlie said, trying to pull away, "Sean will kill Rogan!"

"You don't know that, Marlie!"

At that moment, Rogan flew across the snow, landing in a heap not too far away. He was dazed, that much was obvious, and he didn't immediately get back up on his feet. Marlie wasn't thinking about her own safety now. All she wanted was to save her husband.

Sprinting away from the door, Marlie ran to the gun on the ground and grabbed it. Just as Sean's sights turned to her, she dragged up the barrel of the gun but stood frozen when Sean growled at her. He wasn't more than a few yards away, slowly approaching.

"Marlie!" Noah's voice cracked the air just as Sean charged her.

Her arms were shaking, and her first shot hit the snow in front of Sean's feet. The bear roared, and he was so close that Marlie could smell the stench of his breath. Closing her eyes, she pulled the trigger once more, the kick back of the gun making her stumble.

She waited for the death blow that was sure to come. She knew running outside to help Rogan fight Sean had been sheer madness, but she had to do something. She couldn't just stand there and watch as her husband was killed right in front of her.

But Sean's death blow never came. Snapping open her eyes, Marlie gasped as Sean lay in the snow, bleeding from a gunshot wound to the throat. His eyes were closed and he wasn't moving. Had she killed him?

"Marlie!" Noah yelled again, running out to her.

She could see the other three shifters staring at her in disbelief from the doorway. "Is he dead?" she asked, staring at the large hulk of the bear at her feet.

"Looks like it."

Rogan trotted over to the scene, growling low in his throat as his golden eyes caught Marlie's gaze. She knew he was pissed, and she could imagine the things he was going to say to her once he shifted.

Sean's body suddenly twitched, and he sat up with a deep growl while swiping his paw at the same time, catching Marlie across the ankle with his sharp claws. She cried out both in fear and pain as she stared at the bear in disbelief. What the hell was it going to take to kill him?

Noah didn't falter as he pulled her away from Sean, who was now trying to stand, snarling through the blood pouring from his mouth. Like a flash, Rogan pounced on him, catching Sean in the throat with his sharp fangs. Sean thrashed on the ground as Rogan continued his death grip on the grizzly, not relenting even for a moment.

Only one of them was going to come out alive.

Thirty Five

Rogan bit down as hard as he could. He could taste Sean's foul blood filling his mouth, but he couldn't afford to let go of his throat. His fangs were digging into Sean's gunshot wound, ripping it open. He prayed to God that Marlie had nicked an artery in Sean's neck, and judging by the amount of blood that was already pooled in the snow, he knew his prayer had been answered. Now it was just a matter of holding on tight until the bastard was dead.

Sean was exhausted, Rogan could tell. His own body was screaming for rest as well, but he wouldn't dare let go. He had the upper hand now. Sean was going to die. All Rogan had to do was hold on for just a little while longer.

The bear fell back into the snow, bringing Rogan right along with him. He could feel Sean's windpipe crushing inside his neck, and Rogan's belly threatened to revolt. He wanted to back off, to let go, but killing Sean was now their only option. The bastard must have succeeded in killing the three shifters who'd been guarding him in the garage, and each one of them deserved justice. Not to mention both Marlie and Wade who'd been injured.

Rogan closed his eyes as his thoughts turned back to

Justin, his good friend who'd been guilty of nothing more than being a naïve kid when Sean's fangs had ripped through him, snuffing out his life. Biting down harder, Rogan wanted to take a chunk out of him, to rip out Sean's black heart and feast on it. If he'd been human, Rogan would've had tears in his eyes at the memory of Justin, torn and broken on the floor of one of B*E*A*S*T*'s labs.

There was no way he was going to let this asshole live.

Suddenly, Rogan felt something on his back, and he turned and snarled, snapping at whatever it was.

"Easy there, Wolfe!" Noah exclaimed, holding up both hands. "But I think Sean's dead."

Rogan closed his eyes for a moment to regain his bearings before glancing back down at Sean, who lay still on the snow. The bear's eyes were fixed and dilated. Rogan wasn't prepared for the overwhelming satisfaction that coursed through him in that moment. He took a deep breath and howled, laying his ears back on his head.

Sean was dead. And it was about damn time.

~ * ~

Cops swirled around the house until dawn broke. The neighbors nearby had called the authorities when they'd heard the commotion, but no one had been prepared to see a dead Kodiak grizzly on the lawn. They'd taken Marlie's statement twice, and each time she'd been careful not to mention any of the shifters' abilities. As far as the cops knew, some rabid bear had killed two men and a bird in their garage and had to be taken down by the guns they'd owned.

The police were truly baffled.

Luckily, the B*E*A*S*T* agency had the foresight to weave into their DNA the exact genetic code of the animal their shifters could become, so for all intents and purposes, Sean *was* a Kodiak grizzly, not an insane shifter intent on killing one and all.

It took awhile for the coroner to remove the bodies in the garage, as well as Animal Control to come and pick up the bodies of the animals. Everyone in the house shed a few tears for their fallen friends, the three shifters who'd lost their lives to Sean. Marlie knew it could have been *any* of them in there—Noah, Wade, or even Rogan. She shuddered at the thought and thanked the fates for letting her keep her husband this time around.

Marlie's ankle ached something fierce, but Rogan had carefully bandaged it, refusing to let anyone else do the job. His gentle hands were changing her bandage right now, and she watched him while he propped her ankle onto his leg.

Wade was already healing, his power as a shifter impressing her beyond belief. If she looked hard enough, she thought she could actually see his skin knitting itself back together. But Noah had bandaged Wade's midsection awhile back from torn bed sheets, and he was keeping an eye on him. Regardless of the fact that he could heal fast, Wade was still badly hurt and could get an infection just as easily as the next guy.

They'd downplayed their injuries to the cops, neither Marlie nor Wade wanting to make a trip to the hospital. Wade would never be able to explain his healing abilities for one, and Marlie didn't fancy spending hours on end waiting in the ER for some doctor to tell her to take a few pain killers and stay off her feet.

"You're lucky you were wearing your shoes. You don't need stitches," Rogan said in a low voice, wiping at her wounds with a cotton ball soaked with rubbing alcohol.

Marlie hissed through her teeth. "I'm lucky Sean didn't rip me to pieces," she said with a chuckle.

"That's not funny," Rogan replied, glancing up at her with his flashing eyes.

"I'm sorry."

Up until that point, when the cops had finally left and everyone wanted to be alone for awhile, Rogan had stayed quiet. He'd showered after Sean's demise to get rid of his blood and stench, and he held Marlie close whenever she shed a tear over the night's events. But now that it was quiet once more, aside from the news crew outside who couldn't resist the story of a rampaging Kodiak in a quaint Oregon neighborhood, Marlie knew she'd be getting quite the tongue-lashing from her husband.

"I *never* want you to do something that *stupid* ever again, Marlie." His voice was soft but full of venom.

She bit the inside of her lip and held his gaze, even though it was one of the hardest things she'd ever had to do. "I couldn't leave you out there helpless, Rogan. I had to do something."

"I was doing just fine. You risked your life, Marlie! What if your second shot had gone wide? Then *I* would be the one left dealing with *your* death."

"I'm sorry, Rogan. I wasn't thinking, I—"

"You're right. You *weren't* thinking. I told you to stay in the house, damn it! Why the hell did you think it was all right to throw caution to the wind?"

"I couldn't lose you again," she whispered, staring at her hands in her lap.

Rogan wrapped her ankle in clean white gauze and sighed.

"Losing you once was hard enough, Rogan. If I lost you again, I think I'd literally go insane. I couldn't let that happen. I had to do something, even if that meant risking my own life to save yours."

Rogan said nothing as he stared at her, but she could tell by the look in his eyes that he wasn't pleased.

"You would have done the same thing," she said, raising her chin a notch. "You *know* you would have."

"That's different."

"Why? How is it different?" she asked with a scoff, throwing up her hands. "Because you're a man?"

"No!" he yelled at her. "Because I'm a *shifter,* and I can defend myself. Christ, woman, don't you get it? You didn't *have* to come to my rescue. I was doing just fine!"

"Oh? Is that why I heard you yelping when Sean knocked the wind out of you? Is that why you couldn't get up after he hit you? He was going to *kill* you, Rogan!" Marlie's chin trembled, and she tried hard to keep the tears at bay.

Rogan ran his fingers through his hair and tilted his head back to glare at the ceiling. Wade shuffled into the living room, his chest bare except for his bandage. But the man still managed to grin at Marlie.

"She's right, you know," Wade said, making Rogan's head snap down to look at him. "Sean woulda killed you if someone hadn't done something. I was hurt and Noah was pulling me out of there. The other shifters hadn't even made it downstairs yet. Marlie saw her chance and she took it. Don't be so hard on her."

Rogan growled as Wade gingerly sat on the couch next to them.

"I had things under control."

"No, you didn't," Wade said in a sarcastic voice. "You were winded and on the ground. Another few seconds and you would've been nothing more than a meal in Sean's belly."

Rogan balled his hands into fists, and his knuckles went white. Marlie didn't have to smell his scent to know his anger permeated the room.

"I told Marlie to get into the house, but she didn't listen."

"No, she didn't, and thank God for it. You're alive because of her, Wolfe," Wade said, leaning over to look around Marlie at his friend. "Seems to me you should be thanking her instead of biting her head off."

"Don't worry about it, Wade," Marlie said, patting his hand. "I know what I did was stupid."

"No, it was desperate," Wade replied, grabbing her hand and squeezing it tight. "Rogan's just pissed because he thought he'd lose you."

Marlie looked up at her husband and saw his eyes soften. Her heart burst with love at that moment, and all she wanted to do was fling herself into his arms.

"Promise me you won't do anything like that ever again," he said as he tucked a stray hair behind her ears.

"If your life is at stake, I can't make that promise," she answered.

Rogan sighed.

"Looks like you found a woman who is just as protective of you as you are of her," Wade said with a chuckle.

"Am I going to have to tie you up?" Rogan asked her, shaking his head.

"Oh, I don't know," Marlie answered, running her hand up his chest. "That might actually be fun."

Wade cracked up then doubled over in pain, coughing behind his hand.

Rogan grinned himself. "You okay, Wade?"

"I will be in a day or two. Christ."

Rogan yanked Marlie into his arms and kissed the top of her head. After a few moments of silence, he gave her another squeeze and whispered, "Thank you, sweetheart. For everything."

Pulling back to look into his eyes, Marlie stroked his cheek and smiled. "You're welcome. Now shut up and kiss me."

Thirty Six

"Mind if we take one of the rifles?" Mac leaned against the counter, watching Noah making lunch in the kitchen.

Noah turned around, his eyes wide. "Take it where?"

Mac hung his head and sighed. His eyes were red-rimmed and he looked weary, but Noah hadn't been able to make him get any rest. The three shifters Sean had killed had been some of his closest friends, and he hadn't taken the news of their death very well. Now, it would seem, he wanted to take on the entire B*E*A*S*T* agency by himself.

"Me, Jet, and Trevor want to go poking around in the wilderness again," Mac said. "If that second compound is out there, we're gonna raze it."

Noah stood there for a second, shocked at the bitterness behind his words. "We don't even know if that compound even exists. That scientist Lucian could have been lying."

Mac nodded, pursing his lips. "True, but if he was telling the truth, we've got to know."

"Hey, I have an idea," Wade said, limping over to

the counter and leaning on it heavily.

"What's that?" Noah wanted to know.

"I say we go after that bastard Covington."

Noah sighed and shook his head. "Even if he is *the* guy, Wade, we can't just go attack a U.S. senator. They'd peg us as terrorists and kill us all!"

"That man can't be allowed to continue what he's doing, Noah," Wade insisted. "He's got to be stopped!"

"Don't think I'm not right there with you, Wade, but we've got to think about this. Maybe Mac is right. Maybe what we have to do is look for this second agency and see if it really exists."

"You and Rogan were lucky when you destroyed the compound in Colorado," Wade said. "But I don't think you'll be so lucky a second time around. Whatever security they have will probably have been beefed up on the off chance you'd try it again. And how do you know you wouldn't be walking into a trap? Maybe that scientist is counting on the fact that you'll look for the facility."

"Maybe, but the odds are better than taking down Covington. He needs to be exposed, that much is obvious," Noah said. "But we can't go all vigilante and expect anyone to take us seriously."

"Yes, but once the public sees what we can do, they'll be on our side."

"No, they won't," Mac said, leaning against the counter on his elbow. "They'll see nothing but a bunch of freaks. And that's all we are. The B*E*A*S*T* agency is secret for a reason. If it became common knowledge that shifters existed, we'd only be captured by the public authorities and tortured again to see what we can do! We have to stay quiet and bring B*E*A*S*T* down from the inside out."

"I agree," Noah said, nodding.

Wade sighed and nodded himself, but Noah could

smell his irritation. He couldn't blame him for wanting to rip out Covington's throat. The thought had occurred to him as well. But if the man was as important as he seemed to be, they couldn't just waltz up and kill him without there being serious repercussions.

Laying a hand on his friend's shoulder, Noah said, "Don't worry, Wade. Covington will get his. I think all of us will see to that." Turning to Mac, he added, "Do you have the map Dr. Carver drew before he escaped?"

Mac reached into his pocket and pulled it out, waving it in the air. "Sure do."

"All right. Go ahead and take one of the rifles and the tranq gun. Leave us the other rifle and Marlie's shotgun."

"Sure thing."

"Oh, and Mac?" Noah said, grabbing his arm.

"Yeah?"

"Take this." Reaching into his pocket, Noah pulled out his cell phone. "Just in case."

Mac grabbed the phone and smiled as he walked down the hall.

"You think they'll find anything?" Wade asked with a scowl.

"For all our sakes," Noah replied. "I hope not."

~ * ~

Lanie and Marlie were in the living room talking about their men. Lanie was telling her the wild stories about Noah and how they'd had to keep on their toes to stay one step ahead of Tam, the ruthless shifter that had been after them only a few weeks before.

"Noah just celebrated his birthday last week," Lanie said, smiling. "I even baked a cake."

"You did?" Marlie asked with a grin of her own. "What kind?"

A loud voice screamed from behind them. "DESINO!"

What the hell? Marlie turned to look behind her, but before she could, a blinding pain filled her head with a white flash of light.

Marlie sat bolt upright in the pull-out bed with a squeal, glancing around the living room as she took in her surroundings. Her heart was beating out of control, and she couldn't calm her breathing no matter how hard she tried. She and Rogan had lain down in the living room for a nap after lunch. Now, however, Rogan sat up as well, touching her shoulder.

"Marlie? Are you all right?" he asked groggily.

She glanced at him wide-eyed and swallowed hard. "I had a dream," she said, lifting her palm to her forehead. "Or at least I think it was a dream."

"That's to be expected after what we just went through last night."

Marlie shook her head as realization dawned in her eyes. "No, Rogan, this wasn't a dream about Sean. I… I think I dreamt… oh, my *God*!"

"What, Marlie? What is it?"

Marlie's body began trembling as she stared into her husband's beautiful brown eyes.

"I think I remember Lucian's safe word!"

~ * ~

Mac and the others had left the house a few hours earlier to search for the second B*E*A*S*T* compound, leaving only Noah, Wade, and Rogan behind with the women. All three of them sat around the small dining room table with Lanie and Marlie, who were glancing at each other nervously.

Once Marlie had mentioned the word to Lanie, she'd also remembered hearing Dr. Carver scream it at the top of his lungs before being knocked out herself.

"What's the word?" Wade asked, looking at Marlie.

"Well, she can't say it, genius." Rogan smacked Wade on the shoulder.

"Maybe she can write it down."

"Maybe, but we should test it," Noah said. "Who'll volunteer?"

When no one raised their hand, Wade sighed loudly. "All right, I'll volunteer. Damn it."

"Good!" Rogan said with a grin as he clapped his hands together once. "Lanie, you mind getting a pen for Marlie since she still can't walk by herself?"

Marlie blushed at that, knowing full well she could probably hobble around on her own, but Rogan insisted on carrying her everywhere—even to the bathroom. If he didn't constantly complain, she'd begin to think Rogan enjoyed taking care of her.

Once Marlie had written the word on a scrap of paper, she folded it and handed it to Wade. He opened it and read it to himself. Nothing happened.

"This is it?" he asked, holding the paper up in his fingers.

Marlie nodded. "Yeah."

"Des—"

"Jesus, Wade! Don't say it!" Rogan grabbed the paper from his hand and crumpling it up.

Wade smiled while Noah shook his head. "Easy, Wolfe," he said through his grin. "You're so jumpy."

Rogan rolled his eyes and growled, taking a look at the paper himself.

"Looks like another language. I don't think that's English." He handed it to Noah, who nodded.

"Wonder what it means?"

"Let's go find out, shall we?" Wade scooted out of his chair and walked down the hall toward the family room.

Everyone followed him to the computer, including Marlie, who once again found herself in her husband's arms.

But she didn't complain. She merely wrapped her arms around his neck, content to be close to him.

After a few minutes of searching on the Internet, Wade said, "It's Latin."

"What does it mean?" Noah asked, leaning over him to look at the monitor.

"You'll never believe this," Wade said, glancing at Rogan.

"What?"

"It means 'to leave off, stop, give over, cease, and desist'. Fitting for a safe word, don't you think?"

Noah whistled through his teeth. "Let's test it out loud."

"Why?" Wade asked.

"To make sure it's *the word*," Rogan said with a shrug. "It didn't affect us written on paper, but maybe that's because it needs to be spoken aloud. Fortunately for us, you've already volunteered, my friend."

"Lucky me," Wade said, making a sour face. "Just promise me one thing."

"Hmm?"

"If I do become catatonic, don't go having fun at my expense, okay?"

Rogan chuckled. "I make no promises."

"I'll stay and say it, since you have your arms full," Lanie offered to Rogan. "You and Noah go away for a minute. Maybe outside where you can't hear me."

"All right."

Once Noah, Marlie, and Rogan were outside behind the house, they stood there glancing out over the Columbia River in silence until Rogan turned to ask Noah a question.

"Do you think we can be conditioned to disregard the safe word?"

"What do you mean?" Noah asked.

"I mean, if we've been conditioned to go catatonic,

maybe there's a way to reverse it, so the safe word no longer works."

Noah nodded. "Maybe. Perhaps with hypnosis or something."

The back door opened and Lanie stuck her head out.

"It worked."

Thirty Seven

After a couple of days of rest and recuperation, Wade was like new. He had a few red scars on his chest where Sean's claws had dug into his skin, but he was healed for the most part. Marlie's ankle also felt well enough to walk on, but she still limped everywhere she went. At least Rogan had stopped insisting that he carry her all over creation.

They were all watching Dr. Phil on TV one afternoon when Sean's cell phone began to ring on the kitchen counter. All of them looked at each other in shock before Wade leapt up first to swipe the phone into his hand.

"Don't answer it!" Noah yelled, holding out his hand. "Let it go to voicemail."

"Why?" Wade asked. "The Caller I.D. says it's Covington!"

"That's *exactly* why, Wade! We cannot interact with that man. Not now. Not yet."

Wade made a face and stood there staring at the phone in indecision. After a few rings, it stopped and a red light flashed moments later.

"He must have left a message," Wade said.

"So what are you waiting for?" Rogan asked in an irritated voice. "Listen to what he has to say!"

Wade flipped open the phone and browsed through the menu until he found the voicemail prompt, then he held the phone up to his ear and licked his lips nervously as he listened to the recorded message.

"Sean, it's Covington. You haven't reported in for days. What the hell is going on out there? Do I need to send Brett again? You call me within the next twenty-four hours or I'm going to start hunting you. And you'd better not have hurt that cougar."

With wide eyes, Wade snapped the phone shut and ran his fingers through his hair.

"Well?" Noah asked.

"It was Covington all right. He wanted to know what was going on and why Sean hasn't reported in for a few days. He wants Sean to contact him within twenty-four hours. And he said…"

"What?" Rogan asked when he trailed off.

"He said that Sean better not have hurt the cougar."

Noah looked confused. "Wait, he wants *us* dead, but *you* alive? Don't take this personally, but what's so special about you, Wade?"

"If I knew that, don't you think I'd tell you?" Wade paced the floor before turning back to Noah and Rogan. "Back in Alaska, when Sean captured me, I heard him talking on his phone. He mentioned something about the old man wanting the cougar."

"I remember that," Marlie piped up, hobbling over to where they stood. "That's when I made my lame crack about John Cougar Mellencamp."

Wade smiled at the memory, but it quickly faded. "I have no idea why Covington wants me alive so badly."

"Maybe he thinks you're the only one who can successfully be reintegrated back into the B*E*A*S*T* program," Noah suggested.

With a shudder, Wade said, "God, I hope not."

"Makes sense, though," Rogan replied, glancing at Noah. "You and I were the ones who infiltrated the compound in Colorado. We just picked up Wade from his cell and walked out. Maybe Covington wants to know exactly how much Wade can remember from his life before. They were drugging him, after all."

Wade growled. "Don't remind me, Wolfe. Every time they came to drug me, all I wanted to do was rip their friggin' arms off."

Closing his eyes, Wade tried hard not to remember those times. The scientists at B*E*A*S*T* had drugged any shifter who could remember flashes from their lives before and had scheduled them for reprogramming. Noah and Rogan had come to his rescue before they'd had a chance to brainwash Wade a second time. Thank God.

"Well, what *can* you remember?" Noah asked.

Wade shook his head and sighed. "Nothing great. I can remember bits and pieces of an apartment. I can see the tiny kitchen and the bathroom. And another memory I have is of driving a car on some road, but God only knows what road and what kind of car it was."

"Do you remember anyone specific? Any faces or names?"

"Nope. There's no one with me in my memories. But sometimes, when I wake up, it's almost like I expect myself to be somewhere else. Like all of this,"—he spread his arms wide—"has been nothing but a dream."

"They drugged you over *that* trivial crap?" Rogan folded his arms over his chest, clearly annoyed.

Wade nodded. "Yeah. Some other guys could remember a lot more than I did, so they were the ones who were scheduled first for reprogramming."

"Well, we *do* know that everything we did at that

compound was caught on tape," Noah said. "And I'd be willing to bet my left nut that Covington knows what we look like. Maybe…"

"What?"

"Maybe he knows you."

Wade's eyes went wide. "Are you suggesting—"

Noah held up his hands. "I'm not suggesting anything. But it's possible that he knows you from the compound somehow. Maybe he went on a tour of the place and saw you during one of the scientists' tests. At this point, without knowing more, all we can do is speculate."

"Then what the hell are we going to do after the twenty-four hours is up and Sean doesn't call this guy?" Wade began pacing again. "He swore that he'd hunt Sean down if he didn't get back to him."

"If Sean knew exactly where to find us, then Lucian must have informed Covington of where we are," said Rogan. "That means we'll have to leave this place for sure. Go somewhere else."

"I'm tired of running," Wade said with a growl.

"We all are, Cougar, but we've got to get while the getting is good." Rogan patted him on the back a few times, but it didn't make Wade feel any better.

"What about Mac, Jet, and Trevor?" Wade asked. "We have to let them know there's a good possibility that Covington is going to send more men out here to look for us."

Noah sighed. "We'll just have to call them and let them know. Maybe they can keep a low enough profile so that they don't draw attention to themselves."

"We can only hope," Rogan said under his breath.

"We should leave in the morning," Noah said. "And we'll need to have a full night's sleep if we're going to hit the road."

~ * ~

Rogan's phone rang a few minutes later, making him jump. Pulling it out of his pocket, he glanced at the Caller I.D. and saw that the call was from Noah, so it must be one of the others who'd left with Mac. Rogan flipped open the phone and answered it.

"Rogan here."

"Hey, Rogan. It's Jet."

"Jet! Where the hell are you guys?"

"In the wilderness somewhere. But you are *not* going to believe what we've found."

Rogan's skin began to crawl. Holy shit, had they found the second B*E*A*S*T* compound? He was almost too afraid to ask.

"What's that?"

"A woman."

"A woman?"

"Yeah, and not just any woman. A shifter."

"What are you talking about?"

"It took us about a day to get out to where Lucian's map is drawn, but once we were in the forest, we smelled something and heard someone crying. It was an odd smell, like one of us. You know, that combined scent of a person and the animal they can become. Well, when we found the source of the scent, we found a woman. She tried to shift and get away from us, but her arm is broken, so she couldn't fly."

"Couldn't fly? What is she?"

"A snowy owl."

Every hair on Rogan's body stood on end. The B*E*A*S*T* compound in the Rockies hadn't had a single woman in their entourage, so that meant Lucian had been telling the truth about the second compound. And that also meant there were two other compounds just like it as well—one for each branch of the military.

Rogan had to sit down as he rubbed his eyes.

"Christ," he whispered. "Holy shit."

"Wolfe, what's the matter?" Noah asked, giving him a look of concern.

Rogan couldn't answer him, he merely handed Noah the phone and let him find out for himself.

"Jesus!" he cried out a few moments later.

"What'd I miss?" Wade asked as he emerged from the bathroom.

Rogan looked up and knew his face must be as white as a sheet from Wade's reaction to it. "Jet's on the phone. He and the others have found another shifter."

"No shit?"

Rogan nodded. "A woman."

Wade's eyes went wide, and he fell back onto the couch. "Oh, my God. Then it's true. It's all true!"

Rogan felt a hand on his arm and looked down to find Marlie right next to him with tears in her eyes. He didn't say a word, he merely wrapped his arms around his mate and hugged her close. If anyone could soothe away his fear and uncertainty, it would be Marlie.

Rogan had no idea how long he held her, and he didn't care. B*E*A*S*T* was indeed bigger than anyone had ever imagined. Now he had no friggin' clue what the hell they were going to do.

Thirty Eight

That night, Rogan and Marlie sat down by the river and watched it rush by as a bright moon hung overhead. She was in his lap, leaning back against his strong chest with her fingers threaded through his on her belly. The night was so peaceful that she didn't want to break the silence with talking. She merely laid her head on her husband's shoulder and sighed with contentment.

"What are you thinking about?" Rogan whispered in her ear, kissing the side of her neck.

She shivered. "About how happy I am being with you again. What about you?"

"I'm thinking about where we're going to go and what we're going to do. Noah says we can tag along with him and Lanie wherever they go, but I don't want to burden them for too long. We've got our own lives to lead and so do they. But I don't know how we're going to do that with B*E*A*S*T* breathing down our necks."

"We'll make our own way," she said, caressing the backs of his hands with her palms.

"I sure hope so, sweetheart."

"It'll be hard, but even B*E*A*S*T* with all their

resources can't be everywhere."

Rogan nodded. "That's true enough. But with three remaining compounds around the country, we might have to leave the States. Are you prepared for that?"

Marlie bit her bottom lip and gazed up at the stars. She had no idea when she might see her family or friends again, and that scared her half to death. But leaving Rogan now was not an option. She would die before she left him.

Looking over her shoulder, she gazed into Rogan's eyes and said, "*Whither thou goest, I will go; and where thou lodgest, I will lodge: thy people shall be my people, and thy God my God.*"

"What?" he asked with a chuckle.

He was so handsome when his eyes crinkled at the corners, and Marlie's heart suddenly leapt inside of her.

"Oh, just something I remembered from Sunday School. It's from the Bible—the Book of Ruth. I thought it was fitting." She smiled and caressed his cheek. "Rogan, I don't care where we go as long as we go together."

"What about your family?"

Marlie shrugged. "I'm not too close to my parents, but I can call them on your phone for short periods of time, just to let them know I'm all right. I'll tell them I have a new man in my life. They'll be overjoyed."

Rogan stole a quick kiss. "They'll be pretty shocked to see me when they meet me for the first time."

Marlie giggled at the thought. "That they will."

Taking a deep breath, Rogan hugged her and looked up at the sky. He closed his eyes. "We haven't made love outside yet."

Marlie giggled once more. "No, we haven't."

"You do know my only memory of my life before is of you and me making love under a bright, full moon…"

His words faded away as he began nuzzling her neck. Marlie swooned and lifted up her hand to hold on to the back of Rogan's head in order to anchor herself in his arms. He began to gently nip at her skin, and she couldn't contain the moan that ripped from her throat.

"Yes," she said, "but in that memory, we were in Fiji. It was a lot warmer there."

"I'll keep you warm," he said with a growl, his hands slipping underneath her sweater. He groaned with satisfaction when he found she wasn't wearing a bra. "Your nipples are already hard," he whispered as he lightly pinched them, igniting a fire between her legs.

"It's cold out here," Marlie managed to say.

"Mmm," he said, suddenly licking her neck. "Do you want me to suck on them?"

His hand slipped into her jeans and panties, searching for her moist center. She hadn't even felt him unfasten her pants for all the attention he was giving to her breasts. Her sharp intake of breath echoed across the river as she opened her legs to allow his hand better access to her slick skin. Once his fingers began their erotic caress, Marlie couldn't help but grab a handful of his hair, pulling his mouth up to hers.

She kissed him for all she was worth while he worked her with both of his hands. Within moments, she fell over the edge, crying out into his mouth, desperate to feel him inside of her. Once her orgasm had passed, Rogan quickly unfastened his own pants and turned her in his arms. She had to wrestle out of her jeans, and once her bare skin hit the cold air, she shivered, but whether it was from the cold or her own excitement, she couldn't be sure. Rogan lifted her backside until she straddled him, and he brought her down into his lap, firmly rooting himself within her.

"I love you, Marlie Wolfe," he whispered, making sure she gazed into his eyes. They flashed gold at her while his hands guided her in his rhythm.

"I love you too, Rogan Wolfe," she whispered right

back, leaning into his lips and giving him a kiss meant to tell him there would never be another man in her heart. And she knew by the way he made love to her, slowly and adoringly, that he would never love another woman.

Yes, Marlie's Wolfe was her mate. For life.

Epilogue

Wade didn't think twice about his actions before he grabbed the Hummer's keys off the kitchen counter. He dropped his own cell phone into his pocket along with Sean's phone, then he grabbed one of the rifles propped up against the wall and made sure he had one full magazine of ammo before he quietly walked out the front door.

Rogan and Marlie were down by the river, and Noah and Lanie were upstairs sleeping. It was the perfect time for him to sneak off by himself—undetected. Neither of his friends could clearly see what needed to be done. Clive Covington *had* to be taken down. Not only for the sins he'd committed against the shifters from Colorado, but for the countless shifters that were scattered elsewhere throughout the country. The atrocities of B*E*A*S*T* had to end. And Covington could NOT be allowed to become the President of the United States. Just the thought alone had Wade's hackles raised.

The Hummer was banged up from Sean's rammings, but it was still drivable. Wade climbed into it and turned the key in the ignition. The engine roared to life, and he immediately put it in gear and drove off down the street.

He'd printed out the directions he needed from the Internet maps on Noah's computer, so he knew he'd be able to get himself to Texas with no problem.

Killing Covington, however, was another ball of wax.

Opening Sean's phone, he noticed the battery was almost dead. Setting his jaw, Wade found Covington's number and dialed. It rang twice in his ear before he heard a deep voice on the other end.

"Sean, is this you? It's about goddamn time!"

"No, this isn't Sean, you bastard."

There was a short pause before Covington said, "Who is this?"

"What, you don't recognize my voice? You want me alive so badly, I thought you might have already known who I was."

"Wade." It wasn't a question. Covington knew damn well who he was.

"That's right," Wade said with a growl. "Sean's dead. And soon, you'll be dead too. I know who you are, *Clive Covington*, and I know where you live. You'd best watch your back, old man. Because I'm coming to rip out your throat."

With that, Wade snapped the phone shut and tossed it out the driver's side window as a surge of satisfaction coursed through his veins.

It was going to be a long drive to Texas.

Nature of the B*E*A*S*T* by Rebecca Goings
Coming soon from Champagne Books

One

Somewhere in the Texas desert

"Shit, shit, shit!"

Wade McAllister glanced frantically in the rear-view mirror of his banged-up black Hummer for the thousandth time yet saw nothing behind him, not even the faintest hint of pursuing headlights. His insides roiled and he knew this had to be one of the worst goddamn ideas he'd ever had. Hell, he didn't even have a plan. Laughing bitterly, he drove like a madman through the inky black of the Texas desert.

Sand and sagebrush whizzed past the windows, and Wade realized he had no friggin' clue where he was. No other cars on the highway. Christ, was he even on a highway?

Another shuffling noise came from the rear of the vehicle which had no back seats, just an empty, semi-carpeted truck bed where he'd slept the entire trip to Texas from Oregon. Wade didn't spare a glance at the woman bound and gagged back there, even when she tried her hardest to scream.

"Jesus Christ, what am I doing?" he hissed to himself as he ran his fingers through his sandy-colored hair. He couldn't help but think about all the ways he was going to be killed. And he wasn't even worried about B*E*A*S*T*. If Noah and Rogan ever caught up to him—much less found out what he'd done—no doubt they'd beat him senseless before tearing him limb from limb.

The woman yelled again, unable to move because she was hog-tied with thick rope and duct tape. Her scent permeated the Hummer, and Wade almost rolled down one of the windows for some fresh air. She smelled strongly of fear and anger along with a lighter scent, a feminine one. Some kind of flowery perfume.

What the hell was he doing? He didn't have time to think of her heady scent right now. He'd just abducted Senator Clive Covington's daughter, for Christ's sake!

Another insane, desperate chuckle rose from deep within him. He'd been casing Covington for a week now, and was surprised to find the man had a daughter. It hadn't taken much for Wade to put two and two together and realize that if he had some collateral with the old man, he might be able to confront him with the upper hand for once.

But for whatever reason only Covington knew, he didn't want Wade harmed. That juicy tidbit of information had been revealed through Sean Ross, the Kodiak grizzly Covington had sent to kill Rogan Wolfe. But why? What was so damned important about Wade McAllister? More importantly, if Clive didn't want him killed, then he must know who Wade was—who he truly was.

The assholes at B*E*A*S*T* had abducted men from the United States military for their programs, erasing their memories and turning them into monsters far beyond the horrors of Hollywood. At first, Wade had thought the agency's only compound was the one Rogan and Noah had destroyed in Colorado. But it had soon been revealed through Dr. Lucian Carver, the scientist who'd been captured by Noah, that there was a compound for every branch of the military.

That knowledge had floored all of them, prompting Mac, Jet, and Trevor to go looking for another compound in the wilds of Oregon. And they had been successful—finding a female shifter, no less. But more compounds around the country meant the B*E*A*S*T* agency was bigger than any of the shifters had first imagined.

Noah and Rogan hadn't wanted to go after Covington directly, but Wade knew it was the only way to stop the agency. His being a U.S. Senator didn't amount to a hill of shit in Wade's estimation.

The woman in the back of the truck had stopped yelling and had now resorted to tears. Wade sighed and cursed foully. He tried to tell himself he was doing the right thing. He'd known he wouldn't be able to get to the man who'd funded the B*E*A*S*T* agency on his good looks alone, and abducting Keira Covington had seemed a rational decision a few hours ago.

Wade had been watching her for the past few days, waiting for the right time to present itself to whisk her away. When she'd visited her boyfriend, an anchor for the local Channel 6 news, Wade knew his time had come. The parking lot of the station had a couple of burned out lights, and the guard on duty was an older gentleman with a shock of white hair. It was too perfect.

When she'd exited the building, Wade had pounced, using one of the tranquilizer darts from the compartments in the Hummer to make her cooperative. Once she was limp in his arms, he'd stuffed her into the back, hog-tied her, and now here he was, somewhere in the middle of friggin' Texas with a hysterical woman in the back of his truck. She'd awakened from the tranquilizer not too long before, and all she'd done since was scream her little heart out. From the sound of her crying now, she must have realized her screams did nothing but make her throat raw.

A muscle in Wade's jaw ticked. He'd never done a woman any harm—or at least not that he knew of. Hearing her soft cries, not to mention smelling her pungent scent, reached into his heart with icy fingers. Damn her for making him think twice about his actions!

This was Keira Covington. She wasn't merely a woman. She was the goddamn enemy! Anyone who could condone what that wily old bastard had done to the men in the B*E*A*S*T* compound deserved everything they had coming to them. Even if they were of the female persuasion.

But that didn't stop Wade's belly from threatening to revolt right there in the truck. The urge to shift and rip something apart suddenly reared its head, and he had to swallow hard or risk choking on it. Gripping the steering wheel until his hands went white, he concentrated for all he was worth on the yellow lines in the road

Get a grip, man, he thought to himself. *You'll be okay. Everything will be okay.*

Without thinking, Wade gazed into the rearview mirror once more, right into the bright green eyes of his captive. Her glowing red hair was magnificent, almost like molten lava as it poured over her shoulder in disarray. She was silently pleading with him to have mercy, the terror on her face unmistakable. He damned himself to hell.

Every instinct he had was telling him this was wrong. Second thoughts plagued him as the miles rolled by, and he couldn't help but glance in the mirror every now and again. The woman was beautiful; he'd give her that. But he couldn't let her beauty cloud his judgment—no matter how vivid his memory was of touching her soft, ivory skin.

Licking his lips, he said, "Don't worry, I won't hurt you if you cooperate with me. Understand?"

Keira stared at him for a moment, then she nodded frantically, making her red curls bob up and down.

"It's nothing against you," he murmured, glancing at her once more. "I've got a... bone to pick with your father."

Another scent wafted to him in the truck: surprise. How on God's green Earth could the woman be surprised at that? With all that bastard had done? Wade shivered just remembering the time he'd spent drugged in a small cell at the compound. He could remember bits and pieces—fragments—of his life before, and that had been enough to get himself drugged, putting him on the schedule for reprogramming. Apparently, B*E*A*S*T* liked their experiments not to remember a goddamn thing.

But what he could remember had been trivial at best. The inside of a small apartment. Driving a car down some country road. Was it really worth the painful procedure of brainwashing? Wade shuddered at the thought. He'd been able to suppress his memories for the few short weeks he'd been free of the agency. Now, however, they seemed to be bubbling back up to the surface. Needles and pain. So much hellish pain.

Wade had to choke back a sob. No doubt the woman thought he was some kind of insane whack-job. Christ, maybe he was.

"Shit!" he growled, his eyes flashing. Adrenaline pumped through his veins, making him shake violently. Now there was no room for error. For all intents and purposes, Wade McAllister had single-handedly declared war on Clive Covington.

About Rebecca

Rebecca Goings's first love is historical romance. But she's also been known to write a few contemporaries as well. Becoming a writer has been her life's goal, and she's finally living her dream. Rebecca resides in Portland, Oregon with her husband Jim, and four rugrats (which she homeschools). She fell in love with Oregon at the age of sixteen, and was able to convince her husband to move there after six LONG years in Los Angeles. She doesn't anticipate ever leaving. Rebecca is never at a loss for book plots, and hopes to be around for a very long time.

Other Titles By Rebecca:

On Eagle's Wings
In Your Arms
*The B*E*A*S*T* Within*
Underneath The Mistletoe (in Mistletoe Magic)
Promise Me Forever

Also available in paperback

Celestial Dragon by Ciara Gold

ISBN: 1897261942

When a Deliphit with forbidden powers seeks acceptance, she finds true worth in the arms of a mighty warrior, a man with the heart of a dragon and the soul of a king.

On Eagle's Wings by Rebecca Goings

ISBN: 1897261446

Will Eagle's Wing be able to fix the time-line he's derailed without losing his heart in the deal?

The Confession by Lori Derby Bingley

ISBN: 1897261829

A father's startling confession makes one woman face a past she longs to forget, by trusting the one man who forces her to face it.

Operation Heartstrings by Rayka Mennen

ISBN: 189726156X

In a world of intrigue and conflict, two agents find their hearts linking. Will they escape with their lives and hearts intact?

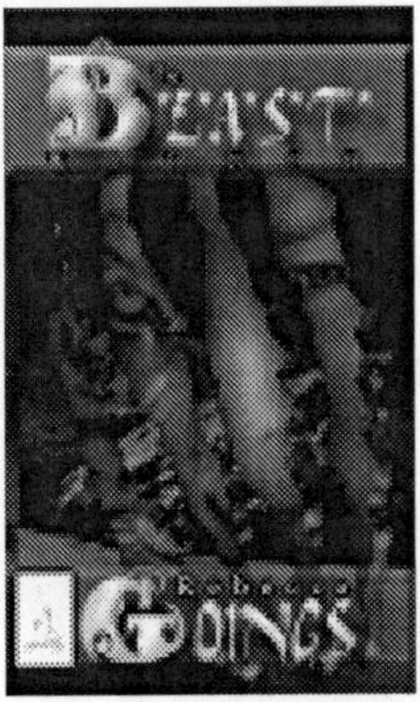

The B*E*A*S*T* Within

by Rebecca Goings

ISBN: 1897261802

On the run, out of luck, and out of time—can Noah save the woman he loves from the very agency that made him a monster?

Send cheque or money order for $9.95 USD
+$4.00 S & H ($13.95) to:
Champagne Books
#35069-4604 37 St SW
Calgary, AB Canada T3E 7C7

Name:	
Address:	
City/State:	ZIP:
Country:	

Printed in the United States
122048LV00001B/28/A